HOW NOT TO BE A MERCHANT'S DAUGHTER

A TRIALS OF AMAFORD NOVELLA
ZACK BROOKS

How Not to be a Merchant's Daughter

e-book ISBN-13: 979-8-9929748-8-1

Paperback ISBN-13: 979-8-9929748-9-8

Cover design by: Susan Roddey

Edited by: Lynn Picknett

Layout by: Jason Roach

Printed in the United States of America

www.zackbrooksauthor.wixsite.com/zbrooksauthor

Dedicated to all of those

who have suffered at the hands of an abuser,

and those who feel as if

they are trapped in an unescapable hell.

You are strong, you are loved,

and you are not alone.

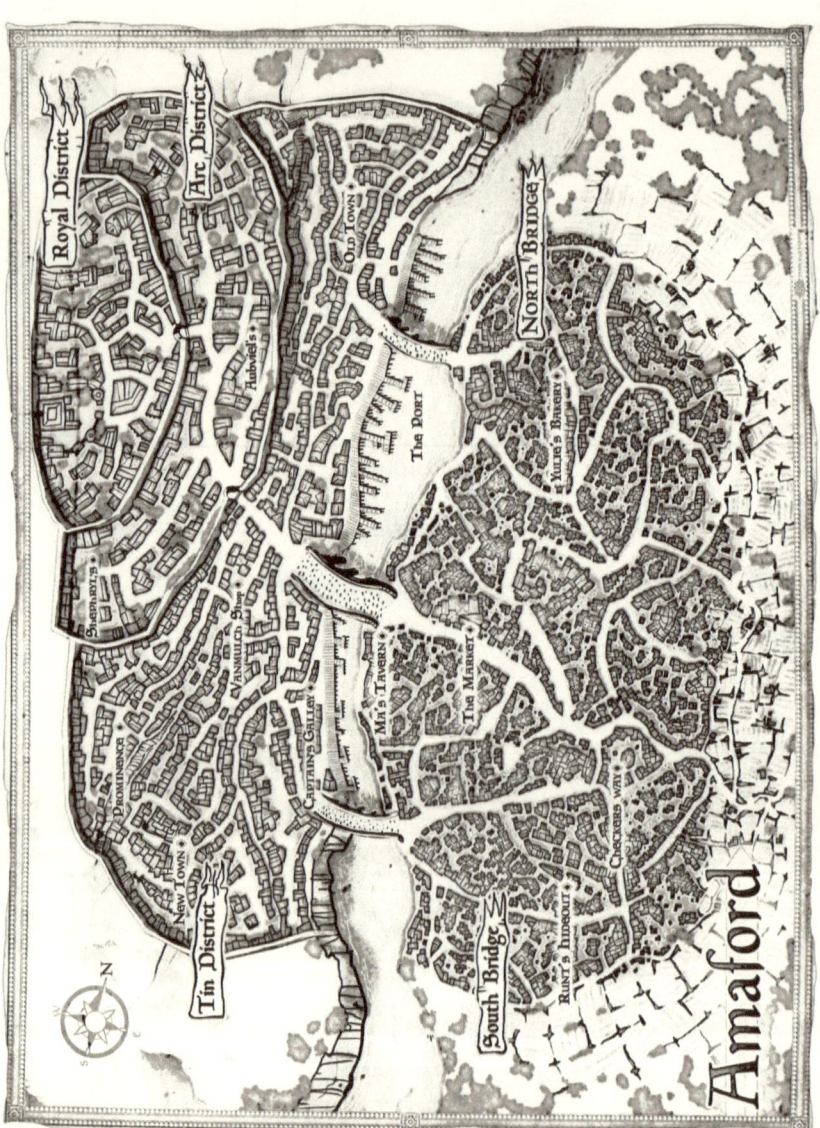

Royal District

Arc District

Old Town

North Bridge

Rothwell's

The Port

Young's Bakery

Shepard's

Prominence

Evanmulch Street

Captain's Gallery

Mr's Tavern

The Market

New Town

Checker's Way

Runt's Hideout

Tin District

South Bridge

N

Amaford

CHAPTER 1

I've never been one to truly fit in, at least not in any other way than how I appear to others, and that's something I've never had a choice in - how could I? It's been engrained into me by my father ever since I was able to walk.

"Keep your back straight. Chin up. Walk as if you are a prize worth winning. Beauty like yours needs to reveled."

Growing up, those words were constantly spoken in an attempt to "normalize" me. There were lessons on etiquette. In fact, they were an everyday occurrence of in-depth instructions on how to properly appear in our society. How to stand, how to sit, and how to eat in a manner befitting a lady worth desiring. It often felt as if the number of tasks I needed to learn were endless.

This was fine when I was young, the chance to impress my father by demonstrating something flawlessly filling me with joy and a degree of pride. But as I grew older, I began to realize the truth. I wasn't impressing him with my accomplishments, I was fulfilling a set of requirements deemed necessary to become a worthy bargaining chip. A simple trophy my father could display and boast about. I was, as he would say, his "rare beauty". This wasn't due to anything I could contribute. No, what it really boiled down to was the shared physical attributes of my lineage, which only became more prominent as I grew into my teen years. But it wasn't the dark hair that was prominent in my father's bloodline. Neither was it my muscular physique, though you never would have been able to tell I'd inherited it from him, that is unless you knew him from his youth. Because my father, like most men of his station aged poorly, gaining weight on their faces and midsections as they lived a sedentary lifestyle. No, it was my slightly too angular facial features and the lack of rounded ears at their tips. All the things that differentiated me from the others in my life came from my mother, who was in fact one of the Elvish people.

Though, for the longest time I didn't know that about her. In fact, I knew nothing about her for most of my childhood. What little I did manage to get out of those willing to risk my father's scorn, was always vague and in quickly hushed whispers. I did eventually uncover that she had originally come from the Englawood Forest, which I've been told can be found far to the east of Amaford. But, beyond that, all anyone ever spoke about was her beauty and how it was something beyond compare. Though, even that I'll never know, as every sign of her existence disappeared after her passing. This was due to my father ordering all my mother's possessions to be sold, destroyed, or returned to her people in Englawood.

Truthfully, I'm not even sure how she and my father had met. I'll never know either, because he refused to talk to anyone about her, and those that did know their story knew better than to speak of it or else they risked upsetting him. Which was never a good idea.

But regardless of how I came to be, it was due to my Elvish features that I became nothing more than a pretty object that my father possessed. Though, I knew better than to think my situation was any different than others, as it was commonplace amongst the daughters of wealthy merchants within the Arc District to be treated as such.

Even on the night of my father's seasonal celebration of the upcoming trading season this was the case, as it had started like all those of earlier years. Those in attendance were elegantly dressed and mingling, while their obedient daughters lingered silently close by until they were addressed directly. The men's controlled laughter was a constant echo that reverberated off the marble walls of our dining hall, and the faux pleasantries being exchanged were done over a multitude of glass tables laden with enticing food. But, for those who attended gatherings like it, it was easy to see some making calculated, thinly veiled threats behind overly

3

courteous gestures. The unmitigated volume of it all made my head throb even as I too was obligated to uphold a forced smile and nod politely to an overweight man that I'd seen no more than a handful of times throughout my life.

Due to his infrequency within my life, I had never cared enough to learn the man's name, and for a good reason. The fine silks and excessive jewelry he wore marked him as someone who often dealt in the warmer parts of Octuna, which meant there was a good chance he was involved with slave trading while using a legitimate trade as a cover. Truth be told, many of the attendees could be presumed to be involved in some sort of unscrupulous activities, as was common amongst the richest within the city. Amaford, being such a prosperous stop on the Kangre River, and the last stop before the Endless Sea, was the perfect place for those with less than reputable intent to set up shop.

The bulbous man before me cleared his throat, which quickly transitioned into a wet cough that sent him reaching desperately for a handkerchief he had tucked in a pocket. The disgusting display snapped me from my thoughts as I eyed him wearily.

"Are you alright?" I feigned concern in hopes that he would have to excuse himself.

"I'm fine, I'm fine," he assured, as he dabbed the cloth at the corners of his mouth. "Now what was I saying... oh yes! I had asked how many seasons are you now? I feel the last I saw of you; you were no taller than my waist!" He began to bellow, his stomach rolling in waves as the excessive amount of jewelry he wore jingled.

"Eighteen seasons," I smiled politely, all while trying to hide the disgust that flooded through me as I tried to block out the stench of smoking weed and stale meat that wafted out of his mouth. The combination of his breath and the sickly-sweet scent he covered himself in an attempt to mask the pungency of his sweat, I felt my stomach turn.

"Eighteen seasons you say! Rither should be considering who might pair well with such a beauty as yourself soon enough." He grinned, insinuating his intent far more than his words.

"Mmhm, father has spent a majority of the night introducing me to 'prospectives'," I said through gritted teeth.

"Is that so? I might just have to have a word with your father tonight as well then." He winked.

I balled my fists within the long sleeves of my gown, grabbing the fabric from within so hard I felt it begin to tear. If it weren't for the lifetime of engrained obedience, I might have just punched him right on his fat jaw. I hated men like him, which included most of the men who attended my father's parties. I hated the predatory gazes of those who believed nothing was unattainable for the right amount of coin. It didn't help that I saw the man's attention constantly drifting downward, inspecting my assets as one might do to an exquisite "product," and it caused an internal shiver of disgust to run through me every time. A disgust so strong that it equaled the rage I held back at being so casually disregarded beyond my appearance. Pair it with the constant similar treatment I'd experienced that night, I was on the verge of breaking.

But, by some god's blessing, my savior appeared in the form of a gentle hand placed on my shoulder, which made me involuntary tense until they spoke: "Vor'Kaige, I hope you are enjoying yourself this night." My uncle's rich tenor voice cut through my apprehension and my shoulders relaxed at the sound of his voice.

Vor'Kaige's dominate demeanor immediately altered as a scowl formed at my uncle's appearance. "Trevan," he all but spat. "I am enjoying myself thoroughly. Especially in the presence of such beauty as your niece's."

"Yes, Aubviel has grown to be quite lovely. Luckily, she has grown to look more like her mother. My brother, like others here tonight, has been gifted with a serpent's tongue. But has not adequately conditioned himself to a lifestyle of restraint." The smile in his tone might have been present, but the slight pressure he exerted on my shoulder indicated that the barb was directed specifically towards the fat merchant.

Vor'Kaige's lips tightened as his body became rigid, or at least as rigid as his bulbous frame would allow. "Yes, and I'm sure your brother wouldn't appreciate the sentiment of those words."

My uncle took that moment to release my shoulder

and step beside me. The bright purple shirt he wore caught my attention as the light reflected off the clear gemstones enlaced within it. My uncle's muscular build filled the shirt, causing it to cling tightly to him and his dark pants were equally as fitting, as he stood towering over the fat man. "My opinion of my brother's appearance is no mystery. Just as my opinion of others is quite public. Shall we touch upon what I think of yours?"

"I ... I have never understood your brother's tolerance of your Fae behavior. If it were up to me, you'd never step foot upon your family's property." Vor'Kaige's face crimsoned as he sputtered out his pathetic response.

Uncle Trevan bent over, bringing him face to face with Vor'Kaige and smiled honestly. "Because my brother knows that my Fae behavior can loosen the pockets of some men more than any woman could dream of."

Vor'Kaige's mouth dropped, and his eyes bulged at my uncle's revelation. The sight broke my dour mood and I had to hide my laughter behind my hand as Uncle Trevan stood again, saying: "Now, you enjoy the rest of this evening's events. I wish to share a dance with my niece." He then turned to me and extended his hand. "Shall we?"

CHAPTER 2

After stealing me away, my Uncle Trevan and I danced for quite a while. Neither of us really enjoyed the parties my father threw, more so because of the company he enjoyed than the actual events themselves. It's not that we had an awful time: we always managed to enjoy ourselves due to each other's company, despite how boorish the gatherings could be.

In truth I believe it's because my uncle and I have always been very close. Even if he wasn't always around due to being sent away on business, making it difficult to see each other as often as we'd like. But when he was around, he was more of the father figure I had always wished for than my own father was.

Unlike him, Uncle Trevan was caring, kind, and stern, when necessary, but never cruel towards me. He was always there for me when I needed him, and that made it much easier to connect with him. I looked up to the man, mainly because he was always true to himself, which is no easy feat when the pressures of everyday life in the Arc District weighed heavily upon its people. It was even worse for us as the constraint of our status within the city was even more pertinent due to our preference in companionship.

"Thank you again Uncle Trevan," I panted, as the musicians took a break from playing and we ceased our dancing.

"Of course, darling. You know I cannot tolerate the men at these things as it is, never mind when a paunchy man like Vor'Kaige despoils my favorite niece's night." He smiled down at me as we walked towards a table for a moment's respite.

"It's no different than any other night within the Chaneze domicile. Besides, it appears that not 'all' the men here tonight are fat clods. Don't think I haven't noticed your attention drifting towards a certain swarthy An'Lin servant," I teased, making sure to look in the direction of the man I was referring to.

The dark-skinned man stood upon the other side of the room in casual conversation, and I could understand why he so captivated my uncle. He was well built with muscle and dressed in tighter fitting clothes than my uncle. Though the brightly colored fabric was lighter and clearly more suited to the heat of the southern lands, the garb was elegant enough not to stand out amongst the ostentatious crowd. Overall, he was a gorgeous man and very much my uncle's type.

"What?" he feigned a horrific expression. "I would nev_-" was all he got out before the veil of his performance shattered and he burst into laughter.

My uncle's laughter was infectious, and I began giggling uncontrollably beside him. We laughed so hard that I had to lean against him for support as our shared humor threatened to send us spiraling to the floor.

"You two better not be having fun without me!" A familiar feminine voice cried out behind us.

I spun at that familiarity with a squeal of excitement, "Sephryl! You came!"

Standing behind us in a beautiful flowing gown was my best friend. Sephryl just so happened to also be the only other half-elf I knew within the city. Her mother, a full-blooded elf from the western forest, Whiteriver Wood, had bedded a master scribe from the Tin District named Padrom VanMulch, who is now known more for his drunken outbursts than his work as a scribe. Pa as most call him, turned out not to be the charming man he once was, having left his scrivener business to his son, Sephryl's half-brother Obis. Who I had met a handful of times on many occasions I'd visited Sephryl's estate, on the other side of the district.

Obis, while fully human, shares many similar traits as his half-sister. They are both lean, with dark hair, and quite attractive despite the hideous nature of their shared father.

Both are older than me by a handful of seasons each, but they'd become good friends of mine through our many outings. I loved spending time with Sephryl: things always managed to become... interesting... when she was around. I always liked how her constant state of curiosity kept those around her on their toes and made her such a joy to be around. You never knew what would come out of her mouth and her blunt nature that offended more than a few pretentious people over the years, I loved. That, and the pursuit of knowledge that never seemed to waver, no matter what the situation, were the reasons we had gotten along so well. Even despite her candid nature, she had been dubbed "The Collector" within the Arc District, as she had a habit of collecting anything and everything that caught her interest.

So, as my friend positioned herself in an open area between tables, one of her hands upon her hip, while still managing to remain poised, she playfully scolded me: "Of course I came, merchants from all reaches of Octuna come to Amaford for this night. Have you ever known me to pass up an opportunity to learn about places neither of us has seen?"

"Well, no…"

"Of course not. Though, what I didn't expect to see is you two giggling like a couple of bed maidens trading secrets about their lady's affairs," she continued, my uncle and I left gaping at her dumbfounded at the sudden brazen display.

Sephryl stared at us for a moment before breaking into a fit of laughter. Unlike my uncle and my display, Sephryl's outburst lacked even a modicum of composure, so much so that there was quite a few openly gawking throughout the room, and she didn't let up for a moment. That was one of the things I genuinely loved about my friend. She was fearless and didn't give a damn about anyone else's opinion of her. Honestly, I had always been jealous of that trait. The freedom she must feel every day compared to the oppressive responsibility thrust upon me by my father. It was that revelation that caused me to frown for a moment, but it was squashed as Sephyrl bound towards me and wrapped me in an uncomfortably tight hug.

"It's so good to see you Aubviel! It feels like it's been forever since I last saw you!"

I untangled myself from her embrace and held her arms as we separated. "It hasn't been that long, only a couple of weeks by my count. Surely you had plenty to keep your attention that long without the need for my companionship."

She smirked and leaned in close to me, saying: "Yes, well I have had something quite interesting come into my life recently. Thanks to Obis I now have a new subject to focus on."

"Oh really? And what pray-tell might that be? I hope it's not anything more perilous than your last escapade. Stalking dwarven Ladies of the Night from the Bridge Districts didn't exactly settle well with your mother if I remember right." My stern expression caused her smile to falter slightly.

"Yes… well there were some very precarious situations that one got me into…" she trailed as her eyes unfocused, and her face went rigid before snapping back to a half smile. "No, this is quite safe, I promise."

"…Well… What is it?"

"Oh! Right!" she began snickering, "Sorry, you know me, always getting lost in thought. Weeeell, Obis has taken on an apprentice recently."

"You're going to make me drag it out of you, aren't I?" I asked, as she just beamed at me in response, and I couldn't help but sigh. "Fine… What is so special about this new apprentice?"

Sephyrl's excitement all but manifested itself into something palpable as she bounced in excitement, hopping from foot to foot and lightly clapping her hands together. "Obis' new apprentice isss… A HALFING!"

My apathy about her reveal must have been apparent on my face because she stopped her fluttering immediately. "What?"

"A Halfling? That's what has you all excited? Halflings aren't exactly rare sights within Amaford. I mean it's true that they don't come here often, but surely there are plenty within the city that have piqued your interest before." My apathy faded as confusion replaced it.

"There's…" she paused and looked up for a

moment, "there's something different about him. Some mystery that surrounds him that I can't help but want to uncover."

"Have you never heard the saying about cats?" I smiled smugly.

"Yes, yes, I know. But enough about my fancies, what is it that's got you two into a tizzy?"

"Well, Uncle Trevan has been eyeing a certain trader's man and tried to deny it." I motioned with a flick of my head towards the man.

"Ohhh." She caught my subtle indication, then proceeded to nudge my uncle while not so subtly staring at the man, murmuring: "You're right, he is quite pleasing to look at."

Uncle Trevan cleared his throat and shied away from her in an attempt not to draw attention to himself. But that plan was quickly shattered as Sephyrl hooked arms with him and waved to get the man's attention. My uncle, the poor soul, was too bewildered to realize what was happening.

"You there!" she yelled across the room.

Realization dawned upon my uncle, and I saw his back stiffen as they walked away. He pleadingly looked back at me, panic on his face and I let out a chuckle while waving to him as they continued their promenade towards the man. The servant, seemed indifferent to the approaching pair despite the spectacle Sephryl was making.

The whole scenario reminded me of my father's

obsession with the idea of pairing me into a marriage that benefited his business. And the gods know he'd already tried countless times over the seasons. The panicked look my uncle wore was the same look younger boys always had when being introduced to me. Though I truly hoped my uncle had better luck than they did. It would always be a losing battle for my father, and the boys were the ones that were dealt the worst of it. In truth, it didn't matter who he presented, I was never going to have interest in men, especially the ones *he* chose.

The encounters only got worse as the seasons passed and the *boys* changed. That panicked look that once dominated their eyes transitioned into a hunger that mimicked their fathers' own ambitions. Years of conditioning transformed them into the predators that "upper society" deemed appropriate for all men.

But even though the situation was a reminder of the atrocities wrought by my father and other men of the district, I couldn't help but smile as I watched Sephryl force my uncle into a comical introduction. Her animated gestures compared to the awkward shuffling of Uncle Trevan was a sight to behold, especially when it contradicted the confidence he usually displayed. Once satisfied, Sephryl patted him on the backside and quickly walked back towards me flapping her arms in front of her excitedly.

"Eeee!" she squealed as she hooked an arm through mine and all but dragged me as she skipped away from the scene.

"You're such a troublemaker," I giggled, her mood infectious.

"Oh, I know," she chimed.

"Where are we going?" I was confused as she began leading us towards the doors to my family's garden.

"Well, I thought since Trevan is now occupied, you and I could catch up with a walk." Her mischievous smile caused me to stop dead in my tracks. The sudden lack of momentum caused Sephryl to swing around and face me, but she took it all in stride as she asked, "What?", worry replacing her smile.

"You really are a troublemaker..."

"Of course, I am! You know you'd never have any fun if it weren't for me!" She beamed once again and resumed dragging me along as we both burst into laughter.

CHAPTER 3

I breathed a sigh of relief as we retreated from the stifling party and into the dim light of the night.

The air, despite the late hour and the oncoming summer warmth, was cool in comparison to the oppressive heat produced by so many people crowded inside. The change was refreshing, and I was thankful to escape as Sephryl and I strolled upon the stone walkway that encircled my family's garden. The area was devoid of torches, and the only source of light was that of the slowly rising late spring moon that had yet to crest the Stern Mountains completely and the glow emanating from the dining hall's large window. The combination of the two intensified the eeriness of the shadows they cast across most of the Royal District.

The Royal District, though not the center of

Amaford, was the epicenter of the city. It housed the dignitaries of the city, Duke, Duchess Aberburne, and their daughter Lady Angelique. Along with the royal family, it housed the Duke's army, visiting ambassadors, and the uncountable number of servants that tended to those within the walls of the district. My father had often bragged about having been there on many separate occasions throughout the seasons, but I'd never experienced it firsthand. I had only ever seen the top of the Keep which towered above the district's walls, its aged stonework enduring stoically the passing of time.

That night, the full moon's luminescence shrouded the Keep in the mountain's shadow, standing boldly as a stalwart representation of the tenacity of its people when shrouded with dark times. Though I'm not sure anyone within the city felt that way, as I had to imagine life outside those walls varied greatly from those within.

"So, what trouble have you made while I've been away?" Sephryl asked, breaking my introspection as we walked towards the garden's entrance.

I sighed, "Absolutely nothing. The most exciting moment in the past weeks was convincing the cook's son that paintings of those passed away harbor their spirits within and they watch over the rooms in which they are placed."

Sephryl stared blankly at me for a moment, before

starting: "You didn't…"

"The very next night, I crept within the servant quarters and began whispering nonsense under the door of his room. Now he greets every painting he passes." I grinned slyly.

"That's horrible!" Sephryl playfully slapped my arm while trying not to giggle.

"Well, not all of us have the luxury of gallivanting through the city venturing for exotic tidbits of knowledge. Some of us are bound to the walls of our home, and one can only entertain oneself so much with books of trading patterns and the brief pleasantries shown by servants," I huffed, frustration making me tense and rigid.

"Geez," Sephryl replied, placing a hand on my shoulder. "Aubviel, I'm sorry. I didn't mean to get you so flustered. I was mostly teasing. Though you should probably save the poor boy and tell him the truth…"

"I know," I sighed again, pausing our walk as my shoulders slumped. "I wish father would get over his possessiveness. It's the Arc District, it's not like I'm about to dive headlong into the Bridge Districts. I'm not daft. Not like you anyway." I ended with a wry smile.

"You cheeky bitch!" Sephryl cried with a sharp intake of breath.

I mimicked her response mirthfully with my own, "Someone's been spending too much time in the Bridge Districts herself. Pretty soon you'll be cursing like a dock hand."

Sephryl broke into a fit of laughter, holding her midsection as she doubled over. The sudden sound of something metallic clattering on the stone in front of her caught my attention and she quickly snatched up the item and she grinned at me.

"What is that?" I asked, scrunching my eyebrows.

She then held up the object and extended her hand out to me and I immediately recognized it as a flask.

She dropped it into my hands, and I studied it as I rolled it over within my hand, noticing its simple design. Its smooth metal surface was cool to the touch and was held closed with a simple stoppered cap. But, despite its plain design I marveled at it. Flasks were uncommon within Amaford, with most of its citizens favoring leather skins due to their cheap cost and ability to hold greater quantities. I looked up at Sephryl with an eyebrow raised and she motioned for me to open it.

I pulled the stopper out, held the container to my nose and took an experimental sniff. The instant the odor hit my nose, I couldn't help but recoil and began involuntarily coughing at the acridity of its contents, almost dropping it in the process.

"Gods, what is that? Poison?" I choked, holding the flask out in an attempt to return it to her.

Thankfully, she took it and its vile contents from my hand before replying, "Oh, it's not that bad. It's a liquor common to the southern deserts. I managed to purchase it from a Keydorian sailor. He told me that it's a combination of cactru water and some root found around the oasis." The side of her mouth twitched in a quick smirk as she pressed it to her lips and took a short pull from it, which resulted in her grimacing and coughing herself.

"Okay, it might be a little bad." Her hoarse voice was proof of the harshness of the liquid.

Rolling my eyes unsympathetically, I ushered her along as we approached the entrance to the garden.

Gardens were commonplace within the Arc District, though, they were usually comprised of a simple motif of exotic flora. But it wasn't uncommon for people to also plant shrubberies, flowers, and even trees that bore fruit, which were meant to inspire awe in those who entered them. My father's "garden" on the other hand, was anything but common.

Where a normal garden might have bushes marking

its boundaries from the rest of the home, ours was comprised of a wall of interwoven vines. Achotl's Hair was the common name for the vines, and it is rumored that they are an extension of the forest goddess' own locks. The vines themselves were harder than stone because they naturally grew so tightly that even a sharpened sword could not penetrate anything but the outermost layers. That's not to say they were without beauty, as one could guide their growth into intricate patterns and shapes. Beyond the wall of Achotl's Hair, you'd not find any exotic flowers from around the world. Instead, you were greeted by nothing short of a miniature forest.

Englawood trees, those my mother's home was named after, grew freely within its confines. Their thick trunks and branches bore large leaves that never fell or changed with the seasons. The ground was a mixture of moss and ferns, as patches of berry bushes and flowers established their presence upon the soft ground. It was as if the small copse was mimicking that of a true forest, so much so, that even birds and small game had made it their home over time. But, while the "garden" was astounding itself, the centerpiece was where the true beauty could be found, as sitting within the copse's center was where a towering willow tree flourished. It transcended the smaller Englawood and demanded that those who gazed upon it pause as an omnipresent feeling of magic enveloped the area around it.

24

When I was younger, I had always wondered why we had a forest and not a garden like the other houses of the Arc District, even going as far as being jealous of those other houses, as I found the other gardens lush and bright colors beautiful in comparison to our dirty and plain forest. In fact, I'd asked my father many times why our house differed so much from those around us, but like most of my questions, it was met with cold indifference.

Once, I had even attempted to rid our home of its hideousness by pulling ferns and plants out of the ground, only to be found and beaten by my father. It wasn't until my uncle had found me crying within my room was the nature of the copse explained. Uncle Trevan, while comforting me, explained that my father had the miniature forest created as a gift to my mother before they were married. He said that, being one of the forest people, she had found herself homesick within the city walls, so much so that she grew uncharacteristically quiet as the days away from her home passed. As they did, her youthful and exuberant nature had become muddled the longer she spent away from the forest where she had been born.

He also told of how my father became quite concerned about the changes in my mother's behavior, going as far as begging her return to the Englawood and her people. He'd hoped that her return might help rejuvenate her in some way. While she was hesitant to leave her life within

25

Amaford, she did eventually agree to pay a visit to her people's home, if only to ease my father's worries. When she was gone, he began desperately searching for some sort of solution and began the project of creating the small forest in a last-ditch effort.

In the beginning, he had a ring of Englawood trees relocated to what was at the time a standard garden. Then, he had moss laid in its center, even going as far as cultivating flowers from the depths of the Englawood forest, planting in various spots. Lastly, he hired a wood maker to create the Achotl vine entryway. It had been a simple thing in the end, and all he was able to do with the resources he had at the time.

When my mother returned from Englawood, the Elven woman he had come to love more than anything, appeared as she once had. In his excitement he presented his project to her, her home away from home as he called it, and she began to weep. Fearing he had somehow distressed her, he took her into her arms, only to find that she was weeping in joy. It was at that point that my parents' love truly began to flourish. Then like the magic of my parents' love, somehow within a few seasons the small circle of trees grew at an unimaginable rate. The vine archway spread, surrounding the miniature grove as if protecting the area. The moss expanded, the flora bloomed, and the berry bushes seemed to sprout up everywhere, becoming plentiful enough to harvest.

But the most magical and surprising gift of all was the growth of the willow. Unbeknown to my father, who had not planted anything of the sort, the willow appeared in the center of the growing copse one day out of nowhere. As mysterious as its appearance, its growth, like the rest of the "garden" continued at a visible rate, stopping only when it had appeared to reach the limits of the vine walls. And it was because of my uncle's explanation of the willow's presence that my view the forest and its hideous creation changed to one of awe and comfort. Because, like my mother, I too was drawn to it, and ended up spending a lot of time beneath the cover of the trees.

The forest, as it had been for many seasons, was where I went to escape the pains of everyday life under my father's strictness. It was also the catalyst that sparked the friendship between Sephryl and I, as her Elven mother often frequented our forest, as it gave her the same sense of peace it had my mother.

But, while neither Sephryl nor I were subject to the same effects of being away from the forest as our mothers, due to our human blood, we felt as much at home within the small copse as we did upon the streets of Amaford. Though, there was another reason we preferred to spend most of our time together under the cover of the willow. It was the one place I knew my father never stepped foot unless he absolutely had to.

So, when I dragged Sephryl towards the center of the copse and plopped us down upon the soft moss at the base of the willow, we did so without hesitation, due to the familiarity and routine we'd followed so many times before. As we did, I instinctively leaned back against the trunk of the tree, closed my eyes, and let out a deep breath.

"It's been too long," Sephryl sighed, as she kicked off her extravagant heels and pressed her feet into the soft moss.

"I know, even I haven't been here in weeks. Father's been up my butt, constantly badgering me about possible husbands. I forgot how peaceful it truly is."

"How are you handling your father's attempts to arrange your marriage?" Sephryl asked, uncorking the flask, and taking a small sip with a grimace.

"It's been expected mostly. Other than in these moments, I'm nothing more than a piece of father's inventory. To be showcased and haggled over for the most benefit to him and his business."

Sephryl's normally pleasant and jovial demeanor turned somber as she looked at me, saying: "And you're okay with all of it?"

"Okay?! Of course, I'm not okay with it!" I shouted, sitting up and staring daggers at my friend. "You know damn well that there isn't, and never will be a man in this city, no, in the entire realm of Octuna that will ever catch my eye. I'm too much like Uncle Trevan."

"Doesn't your father know? I mean that you prefer female companions?" she asked.

"Of course he does!" I ground my teeth. "I might not have scars, but the beatings I've taken for being caught with serving girls were enough to leave me bedridden on a few occasions. That bastard could give a shit less about my preference in lovers."

Frustrated, I placed my head in my hands and screamed. I stayed that way for a few moments as tears streamed unbidden down my face. When I had finished, I lifted my head and continued to stare into my empty hands as I whispered, my voice hoarse with emotion, "I'm no better than a slave."

Silently, Sephyrl sat up, leaned her head on my shoulder and entwined her fingers with mine. Then she spoke in just above a whisper, "I'm sorry Aubviel…"

With tears continuing to fall, I laid my head upon her and squeezed her hand tightly. "It's not your fault, Seph. I'm so grateful for your friendship. Truthfully, if it weren't for you and Uncle Trevan, I'm not sure how I'd survive this at all."

"You're stronger than you think, with or without Trevan and me. Don't ever question that."

After she spoke, we sat there for a long time, Sephryl silently comforting me until I was able to compose myself enough that I could sit on my own once again. Then, as we parted, I noticed her staring at me from the corner of her eye. I turned to see her grinning at me.

"What? Am I that out of sorts?" I asked, running my fingers through my hair in an attempt to straighten it.

"No," she giggled.

I narrowed my eyes at her, knowing all too well that she had something up her sleeve. "Well, what is it?" I snapped.

She lifted her hand and held the flask out to me. "Care to try now?"

"Ugh! You're insufferable sometimes you know! Not a sense of decency within you!"

"So… that's a, yes?" Her grin widened.

Sighing in defeat, I grabbed the flask from her hand and brought it close to my face. I couldn't stop the contortion of disgust on my face when the pungent smell assaulted my nostrils. So, using my free hand, I pinched my nose shut and put the flask to my lips. When I tilted the container back, I instantly felt the burn of the liquid as it entered my mouth. Even as I struggled to swallow the stuff, I could feel its entire progression towards my stomach. The intensity of it caused me to start coughing so hard that I began to gag as I handed the flask back to Sephryl.

"Gods, that's worse than it smells!"

Sephryl laughed and took a swig herself, saying: "You know, it's not that bad after the first one."

"You know I don't believe you, right?"

Passing the flask back to me she said, "Try it yourself, then."

Not one to back down from a challenge, especially from Sephryl, I took the flask from her and threw my head back for a longer drink. Pushing through the urge to cough it all back up, I drank for a few seconds before righting myself and stared my friend down as she gaped back at me.

Smiling, I made to hand the flask back, but I fell into her, the strong beverage taking effect faster than I had anticipated. Both of us burst into laughter as she rolled me off her, and the good-natured mood of the night returned to the juvenile fun it usually was.

CHAPTER 4

My eyes shot open and my heart all but leapt out of my chest at the unheralded sound of cracking wood as something slammed into it woke me. The shock of the sudden noise caused me to sit up suddenly, but the sudden movement provoked a fit of vertigo and the world around me began to spin. So, in a moment of desperation, I attempted to steady myself and cease the chaotic motion of world around me by planting my hands against the ground. To my surprise, instead of the earthy moss I expected to feel between my fingers, I was met by the smooth softness of linen.

Regardless of the unexpected texture, I gripped the sheets tightly, and began employing a technique Uncle Trevan had taught me after one of the nights he'd drunk too much and had all but crawled through the doors of our home. I couldn't help but be amazed by the spectacle and asked how he had managed to even move in his condition. To which he explained in an almost incomprehensible garble that if you found the world getting fuzzy, that you should pick an object or spot nearby and narrow your sight, so it was the only thing you saw. He insisted that by keeping your focus there the world around would become a bit clearer, and you could maintain a modicum of dignity. I found it hard to believe, because as soon as Uncle Trevan had finished his haphazard explanation, he passed out cold on the floor.

So, despite my long-term skepticism, I desperately tried to employ his tactic in that moment. As I did, I was more than surprised to find the room around me came into focus, and it took even less time to realize I had at some point been placed within my own quarters. The revelation left me confused as I tried to figure out how I had gotten into bed, especially since I couldn't remember much else besides the laughter between Sephyrl and I in the garden. Everything beyond that came to me in a hazy blur, and only small snippets of lucidity were thrown into the chaos of the mental fog. They weren't much, only things like the crunch of approaching footsteps upon gravel, a gentle touch as I was lifted off the ground, and a quiet voice chastising me for being so careless. I was in the process of trying to piece together what coherent thoughts I had when my father's sudden shout reverberated within my head, and I cringed from its intensity.

"Aubviel!"

In my defense, I tried my best to turn my attention to him, but the slap that immediately followed his words sent me sprawling as the world once again spiraled around me. The maelstrom of motion made my head swim, and I lost all sense of direction as I reached out beside me, grasping desperately to steady the world once again. It wasn't until I had forced myself to push off the bed and back into a haphazard sitting position that I was able to take a few deep breaths and steady myself. With tears clouding my vision, I wasn't even able register what had happened until I'd brought a hand up to the cheek he'd struck.

Through the stinging pain and teary eyes, I gaped in horror as my father's glare all but bore holes straight through me. It was a stare I had been on the receiving end of many times throughout my life, and just as it always had, the feeling of dread washed through every inch of my body. It only doubled when I realized that the demon, my father's rage, manifested.

The monster he now was, was one that I knew and feared even as a young child. So, I knew in an instant after the slap that my father was gone, and the demon inside had been brought to the surface once more. Truthfully, this was the side of him that I knew the most, and the one I saw the most consistently.

It was his reddened face, bulging of the veins in his neck, and the indiscriminate hatred burning behind his eyes that reminded me of what lurked within him. It was a creature only the house staff, my uncle, and I knew him to be most of the time. And I knew what was coming as I scrambled to mentally prepare myself for the oncoming beating.

"How dare you!" he screamed, spittle flying from his mouth as his eyes bulged. "How dare you embarrass me in such a manner! You knew what I had planned for last night and you chose to ignore my wishes as you always do! Getting drunk with that agitator Sephyrl, IN YOUR MOTHER'S GARDEN, NO LESS!"

I stared at my father, tensing in anticipation, but never looked away. I knew better, learning at an early age that when he spoke you gave him your undivided attention. He had never requested this of the people under his roof: he never had to. Because, once the presence of "the demon" arrived, you had no choice in the matter. Though it was never spoken of, everyone knew not to tempt the wrath of it.

You were not allowed to cast your eyes downward, couldn't look anywhere but in his eyes, or else you risked a physical beating instead of just the berating of his screaming. It just wasn't an option we had. Those that had challenged him in this state were quickly put in their place or weren't seen within the household again. That is, everyone besides my uncle, as I'm not sure my father could stop the man if he had any intentions of disobedience. But, like the rest of us, he'd been conditioned to suffer through my father's moods in their entirety.

It had become such a common occurrence, the rage within my father arising, that I had vivid memories of the times he'd left bruises, cuts, and scratches upon my body. There had even been times when he'd entangled his fingers so deep within my hair that when he pulled his hand away it left bleeding bald spots upon my head. The memory sparked a phantom pain from the now scarred spots that luckily had still been able to grow hair.

The most insane part about it all was that it usually began because I wasn't maintaining eye contact with him. So, I, like many that lived or worked in the house, with the one exception being Uncle Trevan, learned early on that in those moments he was no longer my father, no longer the master of the house. He was the master of our lives. It got to the point where even the staff began to murmur, wondering if he was even human.

But I had heard from Uncle Trevan, and the few staff that remained from before my mother's death, that the manifestation of the demon had been born from the pain of losing her. Because of this, it took many summers before I began to feel as if I wasn't Aubviel, his daughter. I was instead the physical embodiment of my mother's demise, the personification of my father's pain, and he lashed out at me because of it.

"I'm sorry," I muttered.

"Sorry?! You're sorry?! Do you have any idea how much embarrassment you've caused me?"

I began to reply, another half-hearted apology, but his rampage continued and easily drowned me out.

"You simple girl. All you do is gallivant around, taking advantage of my status. You spend frivolously with MY coin. Have I not given you a life of comfort - the clothing you wear, the food you eat, the company you keep? Yet you continue to disrespect me and all that surrounds you. You are pathetic, insolent, and spoiled. If it weren't for the worth of your beauty, I would have cast you out long ago."

The spout of insults persisted as his rage ran its course. Normally, I could manage to mentally shield myself from my father's verbal wrath. But between the pounding in my head, the confusion of drinking, and pain in my cheek, tears ran unbidden and uninhibited down my face as I subserviently received his wrath. As I did, I felt the sting upon my cheek transition to a deep ache, which I knew meant that it would manifest into a dark bruise, making it more difficult to control my emotions. And yet... my father's assault continued.

"- and think of how embarrassed Plendio must be! You knew I had planned to introduce the two of you last night. You knew how important it was for introductions to be made, especially considering how wealthy the Ruldare enterprise is. And to be stood up for that harem bitch Sephyrl -"

"You keep Sephyrl out of this! She did nothing wrong, and how dare you speak of her that way!" I snapped in a sudden burst of emotion at the mention of my friend.

The slip caused me to momentarily panic as I expected him to strike me again. But I didn't regret standing up for my friend, as it was one thing to insult me, but he had no right to speak so crassly about my friend. A friend who had on many occasions helped fund some of my father's more expensive ventures.

After my outburst, I saw my father tense, every fiber of his being constricted, and I knew he was using every ounce of his strength not to lash out physically. "I'm going to let that little comment be forgiven, as you are correct. But if you feel the need to interrupt me again, rest assured that the consequences will be most severe. Do you understand me?"

I nodded, my movements rigid as my body fought against itself. The natural reaction to lash out at the bastard pressed against the bonds of my conditioning. There was a war of emotional responses fighting for dominance within me that I felt as if I was going to split in two. One side wanted to lash out, scream, and destroy the very existence of the man in front of me. But the other wanted to curl up, cry, and wallow in my despondency. The only thing I knew for certain was I wanted this man - no, this monster - to go away.

As my father's silence stretched on, I began to wonder if it had been my interruption, my obvious defeat, or the gods looking blessedly down upon me when I noticed the beast within my father's eyes begin to fade.

He then nodded, "Good." Then he ran his hands across his clothes and patted his hair in an attempt to straighten his appearance.

"You are to stay in and rest today. I cannot risk someone seeing you in this condition. So, you're *not* to leave your room. I will be stationing a maid outside your door to make sure of this."

"But -" I started to protest, the words dying on my lips as my father raised an eyebrow and gave me a warning stare.

As my silence continued, he let out a scoff, whether in disdain or disappointment as he'd been expecting more of my foolish protest, I'm not sure. But, after a moment of watching me, he turned and walked to the door. He paused after opening it, and without turning around, said: "And Aubviel. You need to be better," before shutting the door behind him.

Once the door had clattered closed and locked with a soft click, did I allow myself to collapse into a heap as his suffocating presence vanished. Then despite my exhaustion, pain, and what little was left of my desire to live, I wept.

CHAPTER 5

I felt my eyes flutter as my body began to wake naturally, though I begged it to just let me fall back into the blissful oblivion that was sleep. But, as my mind stirred, it began to replay the morning and last night's events over and over, furthering my alertness. As the memories circulated within my mind, I tried my best to push them away. But every time, it all came crashing back to the forefront: the party, Sephyrl, Uncle Trevan, and especially the tantrum my father had had, all because he wanted to pawn me off into a marriage for his own profit. That's when I felt my body sink once again as a multitude of feelings washed over me, and I wanted nothing more than to drift back to sleep. At least then I could avoid the cruel existence that was my life within the waking world. But I soon felt the sunshine begin to warm my face as it leaked through the shuddered windows next to my bed. I knew if I ignored it, the room would become uncomfortably warm as it left the air feeling heavy, and I let out a groan as I attempted to brush away the damp hair that had plastered itself to my face. But even after I thought I had gotten it all, I felt someone else brush more of it away for me.

Instinctively, I recoiled at the unexpected contact, letting out a slew of very unladylike phrases as I tore away what hair was left remaining. Though, in my frantic escape, I'd forgotten about the bruise my father had left and I let out a wincing hiss as my fingers brushed against it.

Once I'd freed myself of obstructive nuisance, I managed to get a good look at the intruder.

"I'm sorry Miss." The young woman sitting next to me panicked, her eyes darting back and forth, looking as if she was ready to bolt for the door.

I immediately began to relax once I realized who the girl was. She was one of our newest bed maidens, as she'd just arrived at the house a week ago, and I realized this must have been the first time she'd been integrated into the staff rotation.

As she reacted, I was able to get my first real look at the girl, as I had only seen her once before when the older bed maidens had been teaching her the responsibilities of the job. Of course, that meant I had never had the opportunity to speak with her - which was a touch disappointing, as I found her to be quite pretty. Truthfully, she was very plain to look at since she possessed no features that would make her stand out within a crowd. Especially one like the Arc District. But there was a softness about her. Grant it, it wasn't what one would see in a person who'd been born into opulence: no, it was something else I couldn't quite place.

I knew it wasn't the way her light brown hair had been pulled back and tied off in the same manner that the other female staff had been ordered to wear it. But it could have been the way her lightly sun-kissed skin glistened in the light of the sun's rays. Or, it could have been the way I imagined how it might feel as my eyes wandered, following the line of her jaw down to her exposed neck, then to rigidity of her thin frame as it hinted at the unseen curves hidden beneath the maid's uniform. But, as I looked up to meet her eyes, I realized there was something behind her naive blue eyes that spoke of a strength not seen in most of the people I dealt with in everyday life.

"Oh, it's alright." I smiled while waving absent-mindedly at her in an attempt to defuse her apprehension. "I just wasn't expecting anyone to be here. You just caught me by surprise. No harm done."

My tact appeared to work, as her breathing slowed, and the frantic look in her eyes eased, though it was difficult to truly tell, as she still hadn't made direct eye contact with me. Which, despite the norms of others of my station within Arc District, I never insisted on the practice of down casting one's eyes when dealing with others of higher status. I found it to be unacceptable. "…Right. Still, I'm sorry fer startlin' ya, miss."

"Oh, enough of this Miss business. Did the rest of the staff not inform you?" I playfully snapped at her. Though the teasing was lost upon her, fear returning to her eyes.

"N-n-no…"

Realizing my mistake, I reached over and put a hand upon her arm and waited for her to meet my gaze. It took a few breaths, but when she did come to meet my gaze, I began speaking again: "Forget what you were taught on how to act in my presence. I've grown up with the people and children of the staff. And, other than my uncle Trevan, they are far more like family to me than my father is. So please, Aubviel, and for the gods' sake, be at ease. I'm no different than you or your peers."

I could tell she was skeptical about it, but she nodded anyway. Then as if a swine fly stung her, she leapt to her feet, blurting: "Miss- I mean, Aubviel, yer burnin' up" the concern in her voice genuine as her Bridge District accent became more apparent.

46

She then hurriedly grabbed a cloth and submerged it in a basin of water that sat upon the desk beside my bed. After wringing it out, she took the dampened towel and dabbed it gently against my face, wiping away the beads of sweat that clung to my skin. But, despite her tender approach, when the cloth grazed my bruised cheek I flinched and sucked air in between my teeth. The young maid's eyes went wide, and she began stammering an apology once again.

"It's okay," I reassured her, "it's not all that bad. He's done worse in seasons passed."

Her look of concern transitioned to one of disgusted anger and she only hesitated for a moment before responding: "I knew the master o' the house could be…" she paused, a questioning look upon her face. When I didn't react, she continued: "Cruel, ta the house staff. But I neva coulda imagined he'd treat his own daughter the same."

"Well as my uncle would say, 'the master of the house is often the biggest asshole under its roof'." I smiled and she stifled a laugh.

It was at that moment I remembered how precious my interactions with the staff were to me. They were always something I held dear growing up. As some of my best childhood memories were those I'd spent with the staff of the house. This was an uncommon occurrence within the Arc District, since most households treated their staff only marginally better than slaves. That is, except for Sephyrl, her family, my uncle Trevan, and myself.

I couldn't understand the sense of entitlement that was inherent to people in the Arc District. The fact that there were those that took satisfaction in the idea that people of a lower status than themselves depended on them and they chose to lord it over them made me sick. Yet, that self-appointed embellishment only ran as deep as their coffers because, when they found themselves in the presence of someone of greater wealth, they too were treated as nothing more than a splash of mud upon a boot, to be wiped away and forgotten with nothing more than the flick of a wrist. But, having spent most of my life around people who were treated like filth, I saw the world differently.

I truly had more pleasant memories with the people that worked for a living under our roof than I ever had with my peers. I'd loved, been loved, and even admired the common mothers living within our home. Hells, I'd grown up getting into the same mischief with their children as we played together within the confines of their wing of the house. Though most of the children that had been around my age weren't around anymore, having cycled in and out of the residence for varying reasons, I still considered them to be my friends.

It was through these experiences that I learned how

akin I was to my uncle when it applied to whoever caught the attention of my affections. That was thanks to one of the groundkeeper's daughters many seasons passed. But, like most things in my life, it didn't last long as the incompatibility of our stations came crashing down from the master of the house's own hand. The whole thing ended quickly once he had caught wind of it and punished both the staff and I for keeping it a secret from him. But, if I'm honest, the staff suffered a worse fate than mine. But I wouldn't know the extent of that suffering until much later in my life.

So, after an awkward amount of time passed as we sat smiling at each other I finally spoke, saying: "I believe I have seen you before, but I never was able to catch your name."

"It's Fi, Miss- I mean Aubviel."

"Fi... Huh, I like that. Simple but pretty."

Fi's eyes widened in surprise and her cheeks reddened as she turned her head away. "Thank ya. But, how 'bout we get ya a bath so ya can clean up while I have this beddin' sent ta be washed?"

I sighed in faux irritation and started flippantly waving my hand around spoofing a madam of "high society."

"I suppose. I guess one can't wallow in their own self-induced filth all day, now can we, Fi?"

49

She giggled as she stood, curtsied, and studiously spoke, "As you wish, Miss Aubviel. I shall have Dannin fetch the bath as I prepare your things."

She made for the door, but stopped when cleared my throat with an "ahem." As she turned to me, I stood up from my bed, one hand on my hip and a cross look upon my face.

"Yes, Miss?" she asked, concern evident as her posture went rigid.

I mentally prepared my best impression of the snootiest, most pompous "high class" lady I could manage and said, "I would appreciate it if the help would address me by the proper title."

"Proper title, miss?"

I dropped my fake accent and smiled genuinely at her. "When my father isn't around, just call me Aubviel. Like I said, there's no difference between you and I other than what district we were born in." I paused for a breath, then continued with a wink, "Plus, I'm nothing like my father."

As a result of my comment, she blushed once more and quickly left the room. However, it wasn't long after that Dannin, one of the servants that Uncle Trevan had a fancy for, came walking in with a large copper tub, and placed it within the middle of the room. Then he began taking large jugs of water and dumping them in the tub, as I started the process of stripping the linen off the bed, as I had an uncountable number of times before, in hopes of making things easier for my bed-maidens.

Once I had finished, Fi had returned carrying a bucket of Dwarven steam rocks; a special type of rock that retained the heat from where it was mined in the steam mountains, a look of shock evident on her face as she saw the barren bed. That's when I noticed Dannin, who was normally quiet, smiling at her reaction, and nodded at the tub as he had also finished filling it with water. Fi, still caught by surprise, hesitated before she let out an "Oh! Right!" and dropped one of the steam rocks into the tub with ease. Then she looked at me and motioned to the pile of bedding, saying: "Ya didn' have ta do that ya know. It is my job, it is."

I looked at Dannin and grinned, remarking: "She must be new around here."

Dannin gave a half smile, and nodded before scooping up the empty jugs as Fi's face began to redden again.

"It's okay, Fi, there's no need to be embarrassed. I've spent countless hours at Engrid's side helping with tasks around the household." I reassured.

"Really? I didn' know that." She lowered her head, and I couldn't help but grin as I heard her continue muttering to herself as she began collecting the bundle of linen. "Woulda been nice ta know, but nooo, why tell Fi that master's daughter be a saint?"

I laughed and started the process of stripping off the previous night's dress which was now woefully destroyed due to the treatment it had received, both from the garden and a full night of sweat soaked into it.

Once free from the previously constricting clothes, I gathered them all and draped the clothes over Dannin's shoulder. "I'd say make sure this gets washed properly, but it's all but in ruins. And I know what will happen if it gets sent to be washed. Don't think I haven't noticed your 'scarves' that coincidently match the pattern of this past winter harvest festival's gown. Sooo, you might as well just take it now."

Dannin rolled his eyes, knowing full well I was just teasing him. Everyone knew Uncle Trevan had a thing for scarves as "they hide the marks well." It was even something that he encouraged his lovers to wear, since he consistently liked leaving his "mark" whenever he could. Honestly, the fool had more lovers than all the masters of houses combined had doxies.

Fi let out a loud gasp and there was a soft thump at her feet as she'd dropped the linen I'd set aside. This had caught Dannin and my attention, and we turned towards her with a quizzical eye. There was a brief moment of silence as we all just stared blankly at each other. When no one spoke up I let out a sigh and asked the unsaid question. "Everything okay?"

"Uhm, yes mis- Aubviel. Just surprised is all."

"Surprised? About what? The dress? I assure you it will not be money wasted." I replied.

Fi's face reddened once again, and she began looking through the linen bundle with more interest. "Uhm, no ma'am. Just ya, uhm, comfort with bein' around Dannin so, uhm... Bare."

Dannin and I shared a glance just before I burst into laughter. To my surprise, Dannin had even started audibly chuckling, which made it all the worse as I had to lean against him for support.

I managed to collect myself and straighten up before replying to the girl, "Dannin has been with the household a long while. I'm quite comfortable around him. Plus, our strapping friend here could care less about me being in the buff. His tastes are more... specific than me."

Fi stared back confused for a moment, before Dannin finally spoke. His rich baritone even caught me surprise as he said, "I fuck her uncle."

There was a split second of silence as Fi's face paled before she turned and all but sprinted out the door. Though I didn't see her leave as I was too preoccupied leaning on the tub trying to breathe through my laughter.

"That... was... a... vile... thing... to... do..." I gasped, pulling myself into the tub as I wiped away tears from my eyes.

Dannin just smiled, nodded, and left.

CHAPTER 6

I let my mind drift as the hot water of the tub eased the tension and aches from my body. As it did, my mind defaulted to replaying the actions of my father earlier that morning. But, not wanting to relive another of the all-too-common occurrences of his wrath, I forced my mind to stray away from it. Thinking instead of the newest bed-maiden that had just been within the room, Fi.

I began by imagining how she came to be within the service of my father's house. Whether she'd been picked for her skills, which were currently lacking, or if she, like many of the young that went into service for a house, had been out of necessity. To think that one like her might have been purchased from her parents into the service of my house sent a wave of disgust through me. It caused me to wonder how such casual slavery was legal within the city. But the life of a servant varied vastly from those within the slave trades found in the southern regions of Octuna. Still, the whole thing left a bad taste in my mouth.

But if the stories I had heard from some of the staff were true, those whose services that had been bought by wealthy families might have been better off being sold into slavery itself. As some of the families treated their servants even worse than those who'd been forced into it illegally. It all depended on which family whose service they entered.

That trail of thoughts began to devolve into darker thoughts, but I once again pushed them from my mind. Focusing instead on Fi, and how adorable her timidly shy demeanor had been while in my presence. That, and despite being within an unfamiliar station, she was capable of pushing past her own hesitations to perform her responsibilities. Well, at least until Dannin and I pushed our teasing slightly too far, resulting in sending her off in a blur of embarrassment - which brought a smile to my face as I reminisced in the laughter that filled me at Dannin's last joke as I let myself drift deeper into the water's warmth.

As I sank deeper into the water and my own mind, I was vaguely aware of someone entering the room, but I figured it to be Dannin coming back to check on me, or even one of the more experienced maids such as Engrid, who'd been the one training Fi. So, I ignored the presence as I fell further into the fantasies my mind liked to create, which just happened to involve a certain plainly pretty bed-maiden.

So involved was I that when I heard the soft voice of Fi within the room, I had mistaken it for a fanciful recreation within my head. It wasn't until I opened my eyes and saw her standing sheepishly beside the tub that I came to realize she'd been in the room.

At that revelation I felt my face warm, having nothing to do with the temperature of the water, the blush deepening as I realized the irony of Fi being so close while I played out different interactive scenes involving her in my mind.

"Uhm..." Fi spoke.

"Hello again, Fi. I thought Dannin and I had scared you off," I replied, sitting up a touch in the tub.

"Well... I..." she tried to look at me, but quickly diverted her eyes as she saw a smile break through my embarrassment, "I still had ta replace ya linen, and Engrid was insistent I prepare ya clothin' fer the day."

I turned within the tub, draping my arms over its edge and rested my chin on them as I addressed her: "Well, I'm not sure if you've heard. But my father has bound me to my room. So, there's no real rush into getting dressed for the day."

57

"I heard. But I didn' know what ya wanted ta wear. It's why I bothered ya." Her eyes slowly made their way to mine.

"Ah. And what if I told you that I'd prefer not to wear clothes?" I grinned, as she finally met my eyes.

Fi blushed, her face reddening from her hairline to the nape of her neck. "I... I suppose. If that's what' the Miss wishes."

At the use of the title, I tsked at her, standing up as I crossed my arms over my breast saying: "Now, Fi. What did I say about using titles around me?"

Her eyes went wide, and she diverted her gaze to the floor once more. "I'm sorry. Ya're not what I expected when I was told I'd be the lady o' the house's bed-maiden."

"Oh?" I raised an eyebrow at her, knowing full well that she would have heard something from the rest of the staff - but I'd inherited my tendency to tease from those very ladies. So, knowing them, they'd made the girl believe I was some horrid witch of a woman.

"The way the other's talk of ya, I thought -"

"Oh, those pestilent crones!" I cut her off. "Let me guess. They told you I was a cross, particular, pain in the ass?"

Fi nodded meekly.

58

"Oh, ho, ho. This means war!" I said in mock malice.

"Wait, wait! I don' want ta get anyone in trouble." She panicked, looking back up with pleading eyes. "Please don' punish them, Miss - Aubviel."

I chuckled at her response as I held my hand out for a drying cloth. "Don't worry, Fi. The others have made it a habit over the years to tease me by convincing the newer staff that I'm some horrid wench. But it's all a fallacy. I'm no more uptight than my Uncle Trevan's drawstrings."

Fi had been in the process of handing me a drying cloth when I'd spoken. As I finished, she'd stopped, holding it out towards me, and staring wide-eyed before breaking into a fit of giggles.

While she laughed, I took the cloth from her and stepped out of the tub. As I did, I wrapped it around my torso, and wrang the water from my hair over the tub. Once I'd finished, Fi had begun to recover from my quip, her demeanor seeming to have become more relaxed as she handed me another cloth for my hair, into which I bundled my still damp hair in and sat on the bed. Then, I motioned for her to sit beside me, to which she only hesitated for a moment before taking her place beside me.

"So, tell me. How are you adjusting? Judging by your accent, you came from one of the Bridge Districts, right? "I asked, genuine curiosity sparking the question.

"hasn' been that hard o' an adjustment, honestly. And ya, I did. North Bridge, actually. But, after losin' my parents, I spent most o' my younglin' seasons under the care o' Momma K."

"Momma K. that's the owner of Ma's Tavern. The one right across the center bridge from the Tin District?"

Fi nodded before continuing: "She's the one that prepared me fer this type o' work. Me and others like me. It's kind o' what she does. She'll take in orphans from the Bridge Districts and try ta steer them inta a better direction than a life on the streets."

"That's amazing. She sounds like quite a woman."

"She is. She's carin' in her own way. Strict, and takes no crap from people. But she has ta be that way ta keep the riffraff from causin' trouble fer her and the others like me. She's well respected within the Bridge Districts and very few mess wit her 'cause o' it. Especially after Therin tried ta mess wit one o' hers and ended up being boiled alive."

"Boiled alive?" I asked, my mouth dropping in shock. "That's... quite extreme."

"Well, I mean. She wasn't the one that did it. But it did happen within the tavern. Some psychotic gang member tried ta kill her adoptive son, and he managed ta survive by drownin' them in a tub of boiling water." Fi shrugged, the whole thing seeming to not surprise or bother her in the least.

"Is that kind of thing common in the Bridge Districts? It sounds awful."

"Not ta that extent. But the citizens o' the Bridge Districts are no strangers ta death and hardship. It's a completely different world compared ta 'ere."

"Well, I have to say. I'm glad you're here with us now." I smiled and placed a hand on her arm.

Fi, blushed at my touch, but didn't show any sign of moving away and responded, "Me too, honestly. Though…" her words trailing as she hesitated.

"Though what?" I tried to encourage her.

"I don' think I should say. It's not my place."

"It's all right. Like I said, I'm not the mean ole grouch the others have made me out to be. I actually consider myself closer to the staff than I do my own family." I smiled, then added, "Well, besides Uncle Trevan, that is."

At the mention of my uncle, Fi got a curious look on her face, and tried to deflect the conversation by asking, "Does he?"

"Like men? More than he does the wine he drinks."

We both laughed, and I adopted a faux serious expression. "But don't change the subject on me." I teasingly pushed her, "You're more than free to speak your mind with me. Actually, if I'm being honest, I encourage it."

"Oh, okay." She fidgeted next to me before saying quietly, "I really admire ya."

"Oh?" I said in surprise.

"Ya, truly. I 'ave seen and heard the way ya father is, and I don't know how ya manage ta keep sane through all o' it. In truth, it took me back to hear how cruel he can be towards ya. It's not what I expected ta find comin' ta the Arc District. It's like…" she trailed, trying to find the words. "Things aren't all that different than the Bridge Districts. Just cleaner."

I frowned, not for the fact that she had offended me in any way. No, it was the fact that, the more I thought about what she said, the more I realized she was right.

"Oh. Oh, no. I'm sorry, I didn' mean ta upset ya," she apologized, bringing her hands to her face in alarm at how her words had affected me.

"No. It's all right. It's not that you are wrong in any way at all. Just an odd realization. Though, you'd know the comparison of our two districts better than I would. This," I motioned to my room and the house in general, "Is all I have ever known. For better or worse, I make do."

Fi frowned, lowering her hands upon mine as she made more direct eye contact with me. "Doesn' it get lonely?"

Feeling her hand upon mine, I felt my body warm, and I smiled at her in return. "It does. But luckily, I have people who do actually care about me here. They make things a lot more bearable."

Fi smiled back, and I felt a fluttering within my chest as she said: "I hope ya know that I'm one o' those people."

Then, feeling as if I were about to explode, I leaned over and kissed her gently on the lips. For a moment I worried that I had misread the situation between us as I felt her stiffen at my forwardness. But she quickly relaxed and reciprocated my kiss and my desire for her rose.

Taking a risk, I increased the passion of our kissing and was surprised when she pressed herself into me as the intensity increased between us. Things became progressively more heated, and I soon found her hands roaming across my body, removing the now damp cloth covering me as I slid backward on my bed. Without taking my lips off her, I pulled her over me, returning her fervor as we soon were both lost within the pleasure of each other's bodies.

Chapter 7

We lay beneath the blanket of my bed, Fi's head upon my chest as it slowly rose and fell with the rhythm of my breathing. And for a long while I just gently stroked her hair, drifting in and out of daydreams.

Mindlessly, I smiled, remembering the passion we'd shared, and took a moment to revel in her presence. Then my eyes began to close, and I began replaying every intimate detail in my mind: the way her lips felt against mine, the way her body arched when I discovered sensitive areas, and the way her breathing increased in ferocity as our passion played out upon my bed. I was fully immersed in my remembrance and couldn't help my desire for her from rising once again when something *off* brushed against the edges of my perception.

Something or someone was coming. Once I noticed the presence, my muscles tensed, and my nerves felt as if they'd been lit a fire as the world around me slowed. I became hyper aware of everything around me, noticing things I wouldn't normally be able to sense. Fi's breath on my skin caused all the hair on my body to rise. The intense smells of summer, the humidity within the air mingling with the thin layer of brine on our skin, and a faint but familiar sweet scent assaulted my nose. My heart started beating erratically, and its echoing within my ears made it difficult to hear the sound of footsteps approaching. My panic only grew as the footsteps grew louder; the sickly-sweet stench of liquor growing stronger as I realized why it was so familiar. It was the same liquor my father drank.

The sound of my door unlocking soon enveloped my entire world, and even though it had only taken seconds, it felt as if hours were passing as the door swung open. I tried to scream, but it fell dead in my throat once it had opened completely and I realized who was entering.

"Aubviel, my darling niece!" Uncle Trevan bellowed, a bundle in his hand as he sprung into the room even more sprightly than usual, which meant he'd been drinking. Which also explained the smell of father's liquor I'd noticed moments before.

Breathing an audible sigh of relief as my pulse began

to slow, I calmed down because, even if it wouldn't have been the first time my father had caught me in bed with someone, between his recent ire and the consequences of being caught in the past, I wasn't interested in finding out what his reaction would have been this time.

Once Uncle Trevan had entered, he closed the door behind him, and stopped dead in his tracks as he faced me. "Oh… I'm sorry, I didn't know you had a guest." Then he focused and looked harder at Fi, who had begun to stir due to the noise, and smiled devilishly. "Not just any type of guest I see. And who might your friend be?"

"Fi." I answered.

"Fi… I know that name…" He approached, getting a better look at her as he did. "Wait! Fi? As in the new bed maiden?" he asked, stopping at the edge of my bed, then sat before nodding appraisingly. "My, my, you really are my niece, aren't you? Not even the second day on the job and you've already bedded the girl. Good thing I wasn't your fath -" he stopped, his eyes darting back to Fi and gently shook her, waking her completely.

Blinking the sleep out of her eyes, she looked up at him. The recognition was instantaneous and she all but leaped out of the bed, dropping the light sheet that covered her in the process and exposing herself to him.

"Master Trevan!"

My uncle, as calm as ever, gave her a rudimentary glance, looking at her in her entirety without moving his head. Then he turned to me and raised an eyebrow. "Quite plain to look at, maybe you aren't related to me after all."

Fi, gods bless her soul, accomplished something I didn't know was even possible. Her entire body somehow managed to both pale and redden intermittently, as if it were unsure whether she should be embarrassed or frightened.

"I-I-I can explain!"

"There is no need, girl. Whoever my niece decides to bed is no concern of mine. Nor do I judge her on that matter. You, on the other hand, are well within the scope of judgment, and I have to say, dear, I'm not that impressed."

"Trevan!" I admonished, punching him in the arm as hard as I could, which yielded no response.

I, on the other hand, let out a yelp as I felt something pop within my wrist. I cursed at my own stupidity as I always forgot how strong my uncle was, because, despite his flamboyant nature, he'd always been quite fit. Which I guess came with the territory if he was always striving to keep up with the younger men he pranced around after. Not to mention he was no slouch when it came to skills with a blade - which I'd witnessed first-hand every morning he was around for as long as I could safely wield a weapon.

My uncle had taken it upon himself to teach me how to perform multiple different Katas with various blade styles, and in doing so, it became a quiet way for us to bond further, though the frequency of our mornings had tapered off over the seasons, due to my father claiming it was too unseemly for a girl to perform. Even if it was still something I enjoyed.

Fi shrank at my uncle's words, covering herself feebly with her hands as she scrabbled for her discarded clothing. Once collected, she pulled it on and stood meekly with her eyes downcast.

"You may go now, Fi." Trevan stated coldly, his expression uncharacteristically impassive as he stared at her.

Fi, still looking down, lowered herself in a curtsy. But as she did, she glanced up, making eye contact with me and I noticed a mixture of sadness and embarrassment in them. I, in turn gave her a mournful look as I mouthed an "I'm sorry" to her.

"Master Trevan. Miss Aubviel," she bid farewell as she backed towards the door, opening, and exiting it in one swift motion.

As soon as the door had closed, I reciprocated my uncle's foul mood, raising my voice in retribution: "What the hells was that about? When has it ever been a problem for you who I find comfort in? You don't see me barging into your affairs and insulting the himbos you parade around with."

Even though he had yet to turn around, I saw his body tense ever so slightly at my comment, and I knew what I had said hurt him. I still, to this day, don't believe that anyone else in the world would have noticed it. Well, my mother might have, but that didn't much matter anymore. You see, I was told by the older staff that my uncle and mother, despite being of different races, were extremely close. Close enough that their familial bonds seemed that of blood relation and not by marriage. Regardless, the slight's impact didn't last long, maybe a fraction of a second, but it was enough for me to notice.

I knew I should have felt bad, and normally I would have, but I was so annoyed with my uncle. It was completely out of character for him. Well, not necessarily. Uncle Trevan was rude to people on purpose most of the time, often insulting them with fanciful words and backhanded compliments. But those people were ostentatious bores who had it coming. Never had I seen him so... so callous to someone who didn't rightly deserve it. So, what he said next took me off guard.

"She needs to fear you," he said softly.

"What?!" I recoiled, scooting further away on the

bed. "Why? I don't want anyone in this house to fear me, especially not Fi."

"And that is wherein lies the problem. You're too friendly with the help," he stated, turning towards me and put on leg upon the bed.

I gaped at him. He wasn't serious, was he? He knew well enough that beside him, the staff were the ones who had raised me until I started showing as a woman. But to tell me that I was too close to them? What other options did I have? The men of my peers were nothing more than objectifying assholes, their fathers no better, and any women were either pompous beyond help or objectified as much as I was. The staff were the only ones who'd shown me any sort of affection that could be considered friendly.

"Too friendly? Too friendly?!" I started saying, my voice rising as I got to my knees and loomed over him. "What choice do I have? And who are you to tell me who I can be friendly with! You sound just like him!"

Trevan's eyes narrowed as he spoke firmly, saying: "Excuse me?"

"You heard me!" I got closer to him, yelling within a foot from his face. "You sound just like him, trying to control my life. And for what? Power? Or is it that you just can't stand the thought of someone you don't approve of being close to me?"

It was at that point that Uncle Trevan stood faster than I'd ever seen someone move as he grabbed me by the shoulders, pulling me within inches of his face and screamed back, "You think I'm like that abusive piece of shit? Tell me, Aubviel, what exactly do you think would have happened if it had been your father who walked in instead of me? Would it have gone as well? No, it sure as hells wouldn't have and you know it. Gods, Aubviel, use that brain of yours, will you! Why do you think I've stayed here all these years after your mother passed? You think I willingly subject myself to his criticism, his insults, his threats?"

He then paused, and when I stared back at him, eyes wide in surprise, he shook me and yelled again: "Think, gods damn it!"

"I-I-I don't know!" Tears formed in my eyes as I half screamed, half wailed back at him.

He let out a huff of frustration before releasing my shoulders with a shove as he threw his hands in the air and turned away from me. He then began pacing, walking to and from the bed until his breathing slowed, and he stopped, facing the other side of my room. Then, as he continued to face away from me, he mumbled something, but I couldn't hear him.

"What?" I asked, barely above a whisper.

He turned, soul crushing sadness emanating from his gaze as he spoke again, softly: "I said, you."

My heart broke, and the realization dawned upon me almost instantly. "You stay to protect me…"

He nodded slowly and deliberately, as I collapsed back onto the bed. The weight of his admission sitting heavy within my chest as I tried to speak, "I'm sorry Uncle Trevan… For everything. But you don't need to stay here for me. Not when you deal with the same cruelty as I do. Not when you don't have to."

With that, he came and sat next to me, turning my head softly with his hand, exposing my bruised face. When he lifted my chin so we were once again looking into each other's eyes he said "this is why I can't leave. Not while you're still here under his house. I promised your mother to take care of you, and while she'd passed before I could say so, I still hold myself to that promise."

Leaning into him I began to cry, and he pulled me into a tight hug as my tears began soaking into his shirt as I laid my head against him. Uncle Trevan soon started cooing comforting words to me while rubbing my back. This only made me cry harder as I mentally berated myself.

I was so stupid, and I was mad. Mad at myself for

lashing out at him. Mad at my father for being such an awful person and even my mother for leaving me in this world with only my uncle. I let all of the frustration, helplessness, sadness, and all the other negative emotions I carried out through my tears. It was something I did not do often, and when I did, I never had someone there to help me through it. So, I held onto him tightly and allowed myself the precious moment of vulnerability within his embrace.

What amount of time passed as I laid it all bare, I'm not sure. But it sure didn't feel long enough as Uncle Trevan gently pushed me away from him and met my gaze. That's when I realized that he too had been crying in those moments, and my heart lifted slightly at the experience. It's a moment that I hold closest to my heart when I think of my uncle, and it's something I will never forget.

"Are we okay now?" he asked, a small, hesitant smile appearing on his face.

I nodded, wiping away the tears and winced as my hand brushed the bruise on my face. I sucked in air between my teeth I as pressed down on the skin around it, attempting to determine how large it was.

That's when a flash of anger crossed my uncle's face, and he gently removed my hand. "That son of a bitch, gods if he wasn't my brother..." he trailed off.

"It's ok." I murmured, consolingly. "I'll live, it's not like I haven't gotten worse in sparring matches with you before."

"Yeah, but that was an accident. Plus, we both know the risks when we train. This though... this is not ok."

"I'll be fine, don't worry about me. It will heal in no time. Plus, it's not like I'm going anywhere anytime soon. You know he won't let me be seen publicly until it's gone."

"I know..." he replied, turning his gaze down and speaking softly, as if to himself: "I should have seen it coming. I never thought it'd get this bad. Growing up I knew he had demons. But she had changed him. And when she died..." He paused, seeming to fight back tears once again. "When she died, it got worse. I thought he'd heal, thought he'd come back, but I was stupid to think so."

I placed a hand upon him, and he came out of his thoughts. But even though he seemed present again he looked defeated. That's when I noticed he had something gripped tightly in his right hand and I wondered how I hadn't noticed it before. Then I quickly remembered seeing that he'd been carrying something when he entered my room. I'd just forgotten all about it due to our heated exchange.

"What's that in your hand?" I asked, pointing to the object.

"Oh, that's right," he said, forcing a smile and looking at the object as if he too just remembered he was carrying it. Then, he extended his hand and held out a parchment covered package. "It's the whole reason I came here."

"Well, what is it? A gift?" I inquired, taking the package from him, and staring at it.

"I'm not sure what it is. But I thought it would have been obvious that it was a gift," he teased, a more natural smile appearing on his face as I narrowed my eyes at him. "It's not from me though, it's from Sephyrl," he suddenly added.

"Oh!" my interest piqued.

Just before I began to open it, my uncle stood. "As curious as I am to what it might be. I must be going, and you still need rest." He leaned over and kissed my forehead, "I am sorry how things happened today, and I do love you, very much. I just worry about you and your choices sometimes."

In response I quickly hugged him before he could lean away, "I love you too. And I too am sorry. But please, try not to be so… mean, next time."

He let out another smirk and nodded, adding: "I will try."

CHAPTER 8

After Uncle Trevan had left, I'd opened the gift from Sephryl and found it to be a leather-bound book. It felt stiff in my hands, the filthy leather dark, which was only highlighted by the new string that had been strung through its spine to keep it bound. I figured that addition had been Sephyrl's doing, that or her brother Obis', since it was clear it hadn't been the original, especially since the whole thing looked to be quite old. But, as I opened it to the first page, there was a handwritten passage that read, "Though the nights may be long, we find hope within the folds of its shadows." The ink, despite its weathered state, still held up enough to be legible, and there was only minor water damage evident on the yellowed pages. I then began flipping through its pages, when a note slid out and fell to the floor.

Setting aside the book, I leaned over to pick it up and

realized it had been newly inked, though, I didn't even need to see who had signed it to know where it had come from, since Sephyrl's handwriting was almost as recognizable as my own. So, I sat back upon my bed, and read its contents:

"Aubviel,

Trevan told me about the other night after I had left. I'm sorry if I've caused you any trouble. Though it's never my intention, our times together tend to end in strife for you. Knowing your father and his ways, I've given this to your uncle in hopes it reaches your hands quickly. I had come across it not long ago, and after reading it myself, I thought it might give you some hope for your situation. That or some sort of escape during your down time. Again, I am truly sorry, and hope that we can meet together after you've recovered.

Your friend,

Sephryl"

I let out a huff of frustration after setting it beside me. The irritation I felt was not directed towards my friend. At least not completely, since Sephryl should have known she had nothing to be sorry about. She wasn't responsible for my father's actions, and she knew I would never blame her for what had happened after the party. I had made my own choices, and in return reaped the rewards, as unwarranted as they were. There was only ever one person to blame, and that would always be my father.

At the thought of him, I took one hand and gently ran my fingers over the bruise on my cheek, scowling as I felt a sting of pain. My scowl deepened as I remembered a long-time vow I'd made to myself. I had vowed to never be sorry for the things I'd done to earn my father's ire, especially when all his reasonings evolved around fictitious slights that were created within the fragility that made him who he was.

Pulling myself out of my loathing, I took the book within both my hands and was glad that she'd kept me in mind. It wasn't often that I had any sort of reprieve from the prison I so often found myself within. But those moments I did manage to find were always cherished. I then looked towards the wall nearest to the door and reminisced about some of the stories that had gotten me through the dreadfully boring days I had spent in my room. The stories rested disorderly upon a shelf that made up my own little library. The collection I'd accumulated over the years ranged over twenty books in total, but most were purely for entertainment purposes. Standard history, instructional, and books of learning were intermingled within the stacks, but the majority consisted of fictitious stories, poetic collections, and records of inspirational people.

Despite the variety of genres I possessed, it was also

the heroic adventures of men and women fighting against the evil forces of their world that I went back to. I was drawn to their trials and tribulations, their finding of love, and even their heartbreaks that kept me enraptured in them. Those stories were some of the most precious items I owned.

But as I thought about it, the stories weren't the only things within the room that I held dear. That's when my attention drifted towards the first pair of practice blades my uncle had given to me as they sat mounted upon the wall above my shelves of books. The dull daggers were covered in countless notches from their constant use and had long ago been covered in a layer of dust. It was obvious that the blades had long since been retired, as I had grown in strength and skill with larger blades. I now favored the feel of a saber in my hands. But on occasion I still trained with daggers, as it was much easier to carry a dagger within a dress than a saber. The pair that sat against my wall had not been picked up for a long time.

I sighed, suddenly wishing I could be outside, performing katas and sparing with Uncle Trevan instead of being cooped up in my own room. But one must find solace with what one has.

So, I took the newest addition to my collection and sat up against the headboard of my bed. Carefully, I opened the book to its first pages and realized it wasn't what I thought it to be. Instead of a fanciful story, written by a master page, its writing was crude, and not a whimsical at all.

Instead, what I stared at was a journal. Or at least it appeared to be when I flipped through its entirety and confirmed my suspicion. It appeared to be a collection of personal entries, written by the same person. Luckily, the writer had taken the time to note the dates at the top of each entry. So, I compared the first and last entry, realizing that it had been written throughout a twenty-summer period, and the latest entry had been put to page only sixteen summers ago. So why did this the book look so disheveled? It honestly appeared as if it had been around for a lot longer than the thirty-six years over which it had been written. Hells, the book was barely older than my father, for the gods' sake!

"Where did you even get something like this?" I mused to myself, wondering just how Sephryl had come across something in such bad shape, despite its young age. At least in terms of journals it was considered to be young, since most I'd come across ranged more in hundreds of summers.

I was almost disappointed as I flipped back to the first entry within its weathered bindings. But then I thought differently as surely there was something special to it, if it intrigued someone like Sephryl. It didn't take long for my disappointment to completely vanish as I read the first lines of handwritten words:

"I'm not sure if this is a good idea, but Ranette says I should start keeping a journal. That it'll help me keep a level head when dealing in our line of work.

"'Every lady of the night deserves to be heard.' she'd often say to me in what little time we had between the men paying for our company."

I paused in my reading and couldn't stop the mischievous smile that crept onto my face. "Sephryl you cheeky little..."

Then I began giggling incessantly as this was just like her to gift something like this upon me, a journal written by none other than one of the Ladies of the Night that were common within the bridge districts. It showed just how well she knew me, maybe a little too well if I was being honest with myself. Even if I tended to prefer the decorative language provided by the imagined worlds of fanciful stories, I had a strong feeling that I might have just found the most prized addition to my collection.

Once my fit of laughter had faded, I dove in headfirst, quickly getting lost in the world of a woman who'd lived only a couple of handfuls of years before me, in a world only a few districts away.

I wasn't sure how long I was lost within the woman's

story, as it continued to pull me further into her life - truly one of hardships laced with fleeting moments of happiness. She had suffered much abuse, and many nights of wondering whether she would survive to see the next week. But that all began to change thanks to the loyalty and dedication between the two friends. They had managed to change the entirety of their lives, through cunning action and some astronomical risks for two Ladies of the Night.

As the woman's story progressed, I was even able to find similarities between our two vastly different worlds. As we both found ourselves trapped within a life, we had very little hope of escaping, on top of the tyrannical power that held us in place, binding our lives to an existence barely above the value they provided to men.

Her struggles were immense, and even the birth of her only son, which was normally something people would revel in, was tainted by fear and trepidation at how she could possibly provide for the child. It was truly heartbreaking, but one that inspired hope, as she powered through a life that was determined to beat her down at every chance it had.

Sadly, once I'd reached the last entry many hours later, it was clear the woman would not live much longer, and I found my heart aching as she expressed worry over her son's safety: a mother, who'd done her best to save a child from a life of starvation at the cost of her own, a woman who sacrificed her body and mind in order to preserve the innocence of a youngling. It moved me so much that tears came unbidden as I read the last hurriedly written word on its yellowed pages and mourned a woman's passing who I would never be able to meet, or in all likely hood ever learn the name, a woman who was now just nameless saint in a world of filth.

I cried at the world's loss of such a woman and couldn't help but wonder what had happened to the child she had written so much about, the young boy who had given her so such joy, but also fear in her short lifetime. But I realized the futility of it all, and quite honestly couldn't help but think how silly I was for being so upset about something over which I held no sway. Then I recalled how strong both she and her friend were, and I let the emotions I was trying to quell roll throughout my body. I once again let the tears flow freely, as I held the tattered and yellowed leather book tightly to my chest, eyes closed. I let my feelings for the woman into myself, as my breathing came in ragged sobs, and I quickly lost myself in the memories of her life.

As I surrendered to those emotions, my mind began to drift, the world around me becoming overwhelming. When my mind began to retreat, I found my inner thoughts growing stronger as I mourned for the woman and her child. But that's when something odd occurred, something I couldn't even begin to explain, and still to this day have no idea why this woman's story triggered its emergence.

A boy's face began to take shape within my mind's eye: he had what could be described as innocent features, despite his lightly tanned and toughened skin from a life exposed to the elements. His dark curly hair bounced and looked to be plastered back with sweat as he ran through cobbled streets. His clothing, while nothing extravagant, appeared to be well maintained despite his current situation. It was a situation that seemed wholly out of place within the confines of the Arc District, which was easy to recognize, as a guard chased the young boy. As the scene progressed, I could see the boy's lips moving, but couldn't make out what he was saying. Then, a smile stretched across his face as he turned to yell back at his pursuer. But just as he rounded a corner, the boy was abruptly taken off his feet. The suddenness of it caused me to let out a screech of panic, and the visions faded instantaneously.

"What in the hells was that...?" I muttered to myself as I tried to catch my breath while looking around the room but it was just my room as usual. Nothing had changed, and there was no sign of anything I'd envisioned seconds before. It wasn't until I realized I was still holding the journal against my chest, that I loosened my grip on it and held it out in front of me while staring at it.

Clearly, it wasn't the book that caused the vision or

whatever it was, was it? I mean, I'd had plenty of daydreams in my life, especially when I so often had been imprisoned within my own room. But this time it was quite different. It felt as if I was there, as if I had been running just in front of the boy as he scrambled through the streets of what couldn't have been anywhere else than the Arc District. I'd never experienced such a vivid daydream, and that was why I stared at the journal with such trepidation, as it was the only thing my mind could connect it to.

"There's no way!" I spoke loudly, tossing the weathered book to the other end of my bed and standing, trying to create some distance from it.

Then I began pacing the room while I tried to make sense of it all. My mind went into overdrive as I mulled over the experience, trying to recall every detail of the dream, and that's when something caught my attention as I thought of the young boy.

"It can't be..." I stopped, staring at the woman's journal as I tried to recall a detail.

I wasn't confident in my revelation, so I tentatively approached the journal and picked it back up. I held it carefully, since I still wasn't sure if the book was magical in some way. It didn't help that I wasn't keen on experiencing such a vivid dream again. But, when nothing happened, I flipped through the pages, searching for what I hoped was within.

When I finally found what I was looking for, I let out a gasp and involuntarily dropped the book back onto the bed.

"No. No. No. There's no way!" I started saying, almost to the point of hysteria.

The boy I had seen appeared to be around the same age as the woman's son in the journal. He had the same dark curly hair she'd loved so much. But that couldn't be possible, could it? If she'd passed away when the boy was so young, there's no way he could have survived the trials of being homeless within Bridge Districts at his age. Or could he? Was it possible that the boy from the dream had been the same boy from the journal?

"But how... how could that even be possible?"

Just then there was a knock at my door, and I involuntarily let out a yelp as I jumped at the sudden noise.

"Aubviel? Is everything all right, dear?" Engrid's voice came through as I heard the door unlocking.

I let out a nervous laugh at my own childish reaction to the woman and collapsed on the edge of my bed while my mind whirled.

Meanwhile Engrid had entered the room and began clucking like the mother hen she was, nagging: "Aubviel, this place is a mess. And my, you aren't even dressed yet. It's nearly dusk, and you're still parading around in a night shift!" she criticized as she began picking up my discarded clothing. "Come, come. We need to get you properly dressed for dinner."

"Dinner?" I asked, my attention momentarily diverted from the chaos of my thoughts. "Why would I need to get ready when I've been taking my food here, as per father's orders?"

Engrid stopped and stared at me for a moment, "Because he's the one who told me to fetch you for dinner tonight in the dining hall." Then, after setting aside the bundle of clothing, she began chiding further: "By the gods. Fi, that careless child. I'm going to have to have a word with her about letting you push her into neglecting her duties."

Engrid started pulling out articles of clothing from an armoire and I stood, beginning to undress out of routine, even if my attention was still on my possible revelation. It wasn't until she'd tried to hand me a light casual dress that I was brought back to the present situation, and I stared at the garment, before glaring at her. She shrugged in response, explaining: "I had to try. You look so much more lovely in a dress, instead of those cursed trousers you always wear."

"If I'm within my own home, I'd much prefer to be comfortable. You know this."

"I know, I know. But you have a figure of which I could only dream. Wearing these -" she held up a pair of loose trousers and slip-over shirt in disgust. "Is such a waste."

I sighed, snatching them from her hands and began dressing. "Yes, well not all of us appreciate the attention it brings. Now, what has changed father's mind on requesting my attendance?"

"If I had your body. Well, let's just say, I wouldn't be chiding over your hopeless behind." She grinned mischievously at me.

"Engrid, you dirty old coot!"

"Oh, don't even start. Let an old woman dream, won't you?" she cackled before scooping the pile of discarded clothing and placing them beside the door. "As for your father, I'm not sure. I was just ordered to have you ready for dinner tonight. Now come along, you know how he hates to wait."

"Yeah, yeah. I'm coming. Mustn't leave the master of the house waiting," I replied, following the old woman through the door.

CHAPTER 9

I followed behind Engrid as she continued to cluck and pester me about my appearance. This was nothing new, since it was the same old song and dance I'd heard countless times before. So, it wasn't long before my attention drifted, blocking out her droning that had become so routine. Instead, I tried to make sense of the oddness I'd experienced minutes before in my room.

I couldn't help but think that it had all just been one vivid daydream, or at least that's what I rationalized it to be as there was no way what I'd envisioned was anything but a fanciful, if not detailed, fabrication. The concern I felt for the boy from the journal must have somehow influenced me to dream up something so comprehensive. But, even telling myself that, I couldn't help but shake how real it felt.

I'd gotten so lost within my own thoughts about the

whole ordeal that I'd failed to notice where I was. It wasn't until Engrid's loud inquiry shook me from the introspective deliberation that I realized.

"Miss, your seat."

The suddenness of it startled me, and I couldn't help but notice the look of concern that passed over her features as I quickly took my seat at the large dining table, where I'd sat countless times before. Its dark wood had recently been refinished, as it had multiple times before, if only to keep up the appearance of opulence that my father demanded from our estate. It sat on a polished floor, which was constantly being washed and shined by the servants, as he used it often for entertaining clients and guests. But, unlike during the party, the room had only the most simplistic necessities, as the walls were near bare save for the single window that showcased the garden. That and the two other chairs that my father, who appeared to be less than impressed at my behavior, and my uncle sat.

Once I'd settled into the chair, Engrid assisted me in moving closer to the table before excusing herself hurriedly. As she did, I caught my father giving me a disapproving stare but I met his gaze as he spoke:

"Aubviel." His authorial tone provided no room for anything but my utmost attention.

"Father."

"I see your solitary reflection has done little to curb your flippant behavior of late. Mind explaining yourself?" he asked, even though I knew better than to interpret it as anything other than a command.

My father's brashness is what sparked Uncle Trevan to speak up. "Oh, give it rest, Rither! Leave the girl be," he slurred. This indicated he'd surpassed his usual level of intoxication when dealing with my father, and I couldn't help it when I gave him a questioning glance.

"I will do as I please when it comes to my daughter's behavior, Trevan," he replied, his tone leaving no room for dispute.

Uncle Trevan let out a scoff of defiance, but instead of arguing, drank deeply from the goblet in front of him. As he did, my father stared at him: disgust, and disapproval evident as wine spilled over the edges of the goblet my uncle drank from. The whole scene put me on edge, as it was completely unbecoming of my uncle to be so obliviously vagrant. My worry at the sight must have become apparent on my face because when my father turned his attention back upon me his tone was even more impatient.

"Well?" he insisted.

The uncomfortable atmosphere, paired with the

experience I'd had within my room was too much for me, and I fell into obedience by default. I addressed my father's question by lowering my head, but making sure not to break eye contact, murmuring: "Sorry, father. I'd been napping before Engrid came to fetch me. I'll admit I haven't quite recovered from the abrupt awakening."

"Hmph," he grunted, then snapped his fingers, signaling the servants to begin setting the table for the night's meal, before speaking once again: "You'd do well at recovering more quickly in the future, especially once you marry. A wife should never keep a husband waiting, nor embarrass him with such aloofness of the mind."

My father's casual insult was a reminder of his complete disregard for my own feelings - that, and how I lacked any value to him other than being another asset for his accountant's books. A lifetime of underlying rage began to surface within me, as the normal distain that he normally filled me with was overpowered. I had to clench my jaw shut at the rebellious comments that were on the verge of exploding out of me, which were easy enough to quell when the pain in my cheek flared to life as my teeth ground together.

"I'll be sure to remember that in the future," I replied, balling my loose-fitting trousers in my fists as I gave into my father's domineering ego.

"Good, good." His absent-minded attitude furthered my frustration. "Now, let us eat." He clapped, and servants were quick to begin bringing in plates of food in.

The servants carried large platters of roasted vegetables, potatoes, and bread, the usual fare for our dinners. But, when one of the young men entered carrying what appeared to be some sort of red meat, which was most likely bovine as it was my father's favorite, did I realize there was something more to this meal. This was because my father only ever had it prepared for special occasions and notable events. So, when a large serving of the meat was set in front of me, I looked towards Uncle Trevan in confusion. But he was too lost in getting the attention of the serving boy who carried a wine decanter about the room to notice - which in itself did not bode well for my concern over the sudden "treat". This was only made worse as I struggled to make the connection between my father's choice of meal, and my uncle's hell-bent determination to drink as much as possible. I knew the two were connected, as there was never such a coincidence within the Chaneze residence.

So, I turned away from my uncle, and stared directly at my father, my food yet to be touched despite its appetizing aroma. For I knew he had something he was preparing to tell me, though he was taking his sweet time as his focus did not deviate from the meal he'd begun to enjoy. My stomach sank when I noticed the sick satisfaction in his widening smile when he noticed me staring. I couldn't help but wonder if it was the food he'd greedily shoved into his mouth or something else entirely.

"Is there something on your mind, daughter?"

"I was just wondering what the occasion was. Has something happened for us to celebrate?" I motioned to the meal, "It's not often that you're this generous with steak."

The backhanded comment caused his smile to falter for a second, but he recovered quickly as he began to speak: "Actually, there are a few reasons to celebrate."

"Ha, celebrate. Right. Cheers to me then." My uncle raised his glass aggressively at my father, spilling more wine onto the table and threw his head back to down the cup's contents.

My father's attention turned to my uncle and in an overly sweet tone replied, "Now, Trevan, you might want to lighten up on the wine. It won't make your sea sickness any better."

"Seasickness?" I asked, at the same time Uncle Trevan spat "Fuck you!." back at my father.

Ignoring my uncle's insult, my father turned his attention back to me and smiled. "Your uncle will be leaving early tomorrow. As he'll be traveling on a business venture to the southern cities of Kunasai."

"Kunasai?!" I spoke loudly, both in panic and surprise at my father's reveal.

Kunasai, or the Kunasai Empire, was nestled within the only surviving patch of land in what was once a landlocked sea, now named the Acrid Basin. The narrow steppes that sprouted up within the center of the Arid Basin was where the city resided. This was because it was the only place with tillable soil and any access to water for days in all directions. The trip Uncle was being sent on was a two-month journey by sea, and then another two weeks on foot after they'd landed at Potsu Port. That is, it would only be two weeks if the winds held out long enough to allow travel through the unforgiving basin. Traditionally, summer was when venturing to Kunasai was halted due to extreme dust storms that raged for days on end, seemingly at random. So, why my father was sending Uncle Trevan towards the basin at the absolute worst time of year was beyond me.

"Business venture?" Uncle Trevan screamed as he stood, the abrupt motion knocking his chair backwards only to flip and go crashing to the floor. "Don't fucking kid yourself, brother! You're not celebrating any god's damn business venture. You're celebrating ridding yourself of my presence for half a fucking year!" Then he slammed his fists down on the table. "Ridding yourself of your troublesome little brother by sending him halfway across the continent."

"You know as well as I that establishing trade within Kunasai will allow us to expand into an extremely limited market. It just happens that the opportunity is now."

"Bullshit!" Uncle Trevan screamed, leaning over the table, and pointing a single finger at my father. "The only reason you're sending me, is so you can prevent me from stopping your plan to marry off Aubviel, you sick piece of shit!"

"Marry?!" I too screamed, outraged at the sudden prospect.

Yet my father and uncle's spat continued as if I wasn't even there. My father yelled: "Like you could do anything to stop it from happening. What? Are you going to seduce Vor'Kaige, like you would the rest of the dandies within the city? You pathetic excuse of a man!"

When the name Vor'Kaige left my father's lips my body went cold as all the blood rushed to my feet. Immediately after, my ears began to ring, drowning out the continued fight between my father and uncle as they screamed at each other.

Vor'Kaige? I thought, fear running its course through my body and enveloping my entire being as I thought about the disgusting man, I'd been saved from by my uncle the night prior.

Vor'Kaige, the fat repugnant excuse of a man who took satisfaction and coin from the selling of humans, while he plodded along in gaudy jewelry and extravagant clothing. The man who stank of smoking weed and overpowering perfumes that still failed at masking the revolting stench of someone overweight and didn't bathe enough. The man who drooled over me like I'd been nothing more than a piece of meat that he wished to sink his teeth into. Who, if my uncle were right, would become my husband in the near future.

My head swam, and I nearly blacked out as thoughts of what a life beneath his thumb would be like. The stench of his rotten breath on my face as he tried to kiss me. The abuse I would take from a man who valued human life not by its contribution to the world, but by the weight it brought to his coffers. I felt sick and was nearly to the point of vomiting when I thought of the life I would be subjected to as his wife. Desperate, I shut my eyes and began screaming at the top of my lungs in an attempt to somehow release the feelings of dread, panic and rage that had become too much to bear.

It wasn't until I heard my father scream, "Enough!" which was followed by a loud thump, did I stop.

Opening my eyes, I saw his dinner knife still in his hand buried deep into the table's surface. His head darted between me and my uncle, his eyes red with rage and he repeated himself, "Enough! Both of you!"

I stared at the man. No, not a man. This wasn't my father anymore, as the demon within him had surfaced once again and a new fear sparked within me. A concern for the immediate danger that I was now faced with because I knew the look in his eyes all too well.

"This is happening! It doesn't matter what you two think or want. I am the head of this house, the head of this business. What I say is law!" he yelled, then turned towards Uncle Trevan, "You, and your drunk Fae ass will be leaving in the tomorrow. I will not have your woeful promise to my deceased wife ruin our chances at making ties with an extremely limited market!"

Uncle Trevan, whose face was beet red from the combination of rage and drink, stared at my father before taking a page from my book and letting out an incomprehensible scream. Then he stormed out of the dining room, cursing and stumbling as he did so.

After, my father turned to me, the beast ever present in his eyes as he smiled crookedly. "And you, young lady. As Trevan has revealed, will be wed to Vor'Kaige Crerril in the next month. Your marriage will strengthen the connections we will be making to the empire - and no, you do not have a choice in the matter. You will be compliant, despite your feelings towards the man."

I stood, staring at the monster before me, unable to speak: my mind and body had been rendered useless as the shock of it all set in. As I did, my father spoke once again: "I suppose I should thank you and your uncle for this turn of fortune. If it hadn't been for your memorable interactions with Vor'Kaige, he never would have approached me the other night. So, if you want to blame anyone for your current situations and futures, you should really turn your attention to yourselves."

He then let go of the knife and began brushing his clothing off, straightening himself, and added: "Now. Since this meal has been fully ruined, I have a meeting to attend."

On cue, one of the serving boys rushed in behind him and pulled out his chair, allowing him to step aside as he fixed the sleeves of his shirt. "Enjoy the rest of your night, daughter, we've much conditioning for you to undergo before I hand you over." He grinned evilly, while turning to leave. "I will very much enjoy breaking you of your..." he paused, appearing to fail at finding the correct words. Then nodded: "Bad habits."

My father excused himself, and when paired with my uncle's abrupt exit, I found myself alone in a place somewhere between rage and terror, while the servants flitted about the room. But, even with them around, there was a silence that hung in the air that was only broken by the sound of footsteps and the quivering of the knife my father had stabbed into the table. Then, once again, the entirety of what had just happened hit me all at once, and I collapsed into my chair weeping openly.

It wasn't until I felt a hand on my shoulder, and a quiet whisper from Engrid did I begin to move. "Miss Aubviel. Please, let me help you to your room."

I allowed the older woman to help me rise, and mindlessly followed her as she guided me out of the room. But, when we were stepping into the hallway, I paused, staring at the other servants while they quietly started to clean the chaos that my family had left. The sight caused tears to form at the edges of my eyes, and the world became a blurry mess once I realized my life had just been ripped apart.

CHAPTER 10

Engrid and I soon entered my room, and she guided me to where the armoire contained most of my clothing. I was incapable of doing anything but stand there in silence as tears continued to run down my cheeks even after I'd consciously stopped crying. I was unable to stop them even if I wanted to all while a single name replayed over and over in my mind.

'Vor'Kaige.'

The name caused a complete numbness to engulf me and it blanketed my broken spirit from the horrors of my soon to be reality. I allowed myself to devolve into a series of dark thoughts – even thoughts of taking my own life, since it would be a better alternative than subjecting myself to the torturous life I was in store for at the hands of that man.

Then I began playing out the diverse ways I would be able to do so.

I thought of the daggers upon my wall but dismissed them as they had been dulled with age, then of the countless smaller blades I had within my room and how easy it would be to open the veins in my wrists. Countless scenarios passed through my head, each ending with a single goal in mind, making sure that however I did it, I would be sure that my father knew exactly who was responsible for my actions. Him. It was the only way I felt I could take back control of what was left of my life. In doing so, I'd make sure that no man was allowed to force their will upon me ever again.

These thoughts continued to cycle through me in a whirlwind, even as Engrid began the process of undressing me. But I didn't feel her, didn't see anything but the ways I could enact revenge on the monster that was my father. I didn't hear her quiet attempts to soothe me with words of encouragement to hang on. I didn't notice as she guided me to my bed, pulling back the covers, and allowed me to lie beneath them. I didn't notice as she left the room, closing the door gently behind her as tears ran down her weathered face. It didn't matter, nothing mattered in those moments. Nothing but the death I so rightly wanted.

So lost was I, that when the door opened again, I didn't see or hear Fi enter the room. Nor did I notice when she approached, pulling the covers aside and sliding into bed with me and resting her head across my stomach. I was incapable of feeling, incapable of reacting to someone who'd excited and dominated my thoughts hours earlier. It wasn't if I didn't want to. Gods, all I wanted to do was hold her tight and cry my pain away within her embrace. I truthfully would have given anything to leave the world behind and fill it completely with her presence. But I couldn't.

All I was capable of doing was lying there, while the girl who I was so sure could bring some assemblance of happiness to my ill-begotten life, attempted to comfort me. Instead, I stared at the darkened ceiling as candlelight flickered across its surface.

Eventually, my mind, like my body, had become numb as I got lost within the erratic patterns of shadows cast by the flickering flame. I fell deep into their chaos as I breathed deeply, barely hearing Fi's soft snoring as an inexplicable amount of time had passed.

Then, slowly, ever so slowly, the feeling of hopelessness and despair began to pass. As it did, I felt the weight of Fi upon my chest, felt the subtle way her body rose and fell as our breathing oddly matched. Soon after, my emotions relinquished their hold over my body, and I gently turned my head to see the plainly beautiful girl who'd come to ease my pain. My heart broke as I realized our time was limited, and that in the not so far future, these possibilities would soon become impossible. So, I softly rested my hand on her and focused all my will on enjoying this simple and touching moment. As I did, I tentatively let my mind drift once again.

What came to mind was not what I had expected, as it drifted towards thoughts of my uncle. My poor uncle, who'd suffered just as much abuse from my father as I had since my mother's death. Uncle Trevan, who had done nothing but do his best to keep me safe and happy while still enjoying a simpler life filled with passion. It was then that my heart broke for a second time, as I realized tonight was the last night I'd probably ever see my beloved uncle again.

Because of this, I began picturing him in detail. The way his body was poised and relaxed, the way he grinned through his sweat-laden brow while we both put our all into a sparring match. From his short, cropped hair, to the painstaking way he picked out his outfits to best show off his muscular body. All the way down to the way he laughed at crude jokes, or teased people in a way to make them smile. Because of this, paired with Fi's rhythmic breathing, I soon found the world fading around me and slowly an image of my uncle sprawled haphazardly inside what appeared to be a carriage formed.

At first, I was surprised, but held onto the sight of him. In doing so, the image of him became stronger. Eventually, I noticed how his body bounced as he half lay, half sat upon

106

a padded bench while the carriage proceeded despite his current state. Instantly, I realized what was happening, and instead of pulling away as with the vision of the boy, I focused harder on the scene around me. In doing so, I found that the harder I focused, the more detail was revealed: things like the sound of my uncle loud snoring, the clack of a horse's hooves on the cobbled streets, and the constant creaking of the wooden carriage's movement. I even noticed the sharp acidic smell of vomit, wine, and the lingering scent of my uncle's perfume.

I reveled in the wonder of it all and wanted nothing more than to wake my sleeping uncle to tell him all about what was happening to me. But no matter how hard I tried, I was not able to interact with him. I was an invisible passenger, unable to influence what was occurring in my mind. So, I stayed within that space a while, trying to mentally manipulate the surroundings I was seeing. But it was all for nothing, because after a couple of minutes my frustration got the better of me, and the vision began to fade.

As it did, my room came back into focus before my eyes. In fact, all my senses returned to me: the feeling of Fi sleeping upon me, the bed beneath me, and even the slight summer breeze that blew through the window beside us. Even the scents of my room and home gently came back. The transition was nowhere as sudden as the time before, for which I was grateful. But I couldn't help but realize that what

I thought I was imagining earlier that day might not have been the case.

The more I thought about it, the more curious I became if I could replicate it.

So, I attempted to trigger the visions once more. focusing on my Fi and my breathing while letting my body relax as I fell into the comforting rhythm it provided. I allowed my mind to drift, focusing upon the first person to appear - which happened to be my father, because, despite the calm I felt, I still had a burning rage that always roiled deep within me directed towards the man. Then I started picturing every horrid feature, every mannerism, and all the hateful emotions I kept buried within myself for my father surface.

This time, the world didn't slowly fade, revealing something new. No, the scene within my mind immediately snapped into focus. The images, sounds, and smells assaulted me all at once, and I barely hung on to the vision as it shocked my system. But, once I acclimated to changes, the actions that played out are what sent my life spiraling in a direction I could never have imagined.

CHAPTER 11

Once I had adjusted, a few things were made obvious.

My father was in a location far from our house, which was clear due to constant scraping of wood upon wood and the horrid stench of old fish, muddied brine of river water, and damp hay. He was obviously somewhere near the river's edge and possibly near enough to the port that the endless array of boats and barges could be heard through the room's flimsy walls. Walls that were so dingy that I could see parts of the wood displaying signs of rot as black spots littered the interior. Even the floor looked like it was ready to buckle if it was to bear too much weight.

Within that death trap of a room there was a simple desk, with next to nothing on it, except for a pair of gold stitched boots that rested casually atop its surface and were being worn by a leanly muscles woman with olive skin, and black hair, who reclined carelessly back in a wooden chair. There was also a terrifyingly rough-looking man who leaned casually against one of the cleaner areas of the wall. Then, as I inspected him further, I could tell that despite his relaxed appearance, he was capable of reacting with ease to any situation that would arise.

My father, who stood across from the pair, displayed a demeanor that I'd never seen before. And it wasn't until I saw his hands begin to fidget with the cuffs of his shirt, that I realized what the foreign mannerisms were. My father was nervous. Regardless of his alien mood, I still wanted nothing more than to scream at him, berating him for all he had done to that point. But, as I could do nothing, I mentally glared at the man.

What in the hells are you doing that would make a monster like you nervous? I thought. But that was before the woman began to speak, and it became quite obvious.

"Rither, it's been a while." Her tone, like the man's demeanor, was relaxed, but insinuated that she had more than enough power to crush my father where he stood.

"I beg your pardon, Jazmin, as I must apologize for coming here on such short notice. But, after our last meeting fell through, the timetable of my request has shortened significantly."

"Yes, I must confess, something had come up that took precedence over our meeting." She paused, noticing my father tense in irritation, and raised an eyebrow as the corner of her mouth lifted into a smirk. "Someone who stands much higher than yourself on our priority list."

I could tell by the sudden change in father's demeanor that he wanted to argue and berate the woman for what he clearly thought was an insult. But as he opened his mouth, the man leaning upon the wall walked forward to stand beside Jazmin. My father quickly shut his mouth, and I noticed that he involuntarily took a step away from the pair.

This brought a wide smile to Jazmin's face, and she waved a clawed hand at the man. "Lohan, it's not polite to intimidate our guests and potential clients."

"Sorry, Jaz." Clearly feeling no remorse for the action.

"Oh. Don't apologize to me. It's Rither that you should be saying sorry to. Look at him, he's all but pissing himself now. And that is no way to start a business transaction."

"Right," he replied, without taking his eyes off my father, before adding an emotionless "Sorry."

My father tensed further, as Jazmin swung her legs off the desk and sat straight, her clawed fingers tapping its surface. "Now, please tell us, what does such a mediocre merchant like yourself require from us that warrants such last-minute notice?"

"Yes, well, after our last meeting was -" my father began but was interrupted as Jazmin dragged her claws across the desk, immediately silencing him.

"Rither, Rither, Rither. I let the first indignation go as it was warranted since we were responsible for the sudden change in plans. But…" she paused, holding up her hand and inspecting the sharpened points on each of her fingers. "If you insist on showing further opprobrium, you will find my patience begin to wane."

"I-I-I apologize, it won't happen again, Jazmin," my father stuttered, highlighting the fear he was barely holding back.

"Good. You may proceed then."

"Yes… Thank you," he replied, straightening himself and his clothing in an attempt to appear more put together. "The reason I have come here on such short notice is that I require you and your… men to solve a problem for me. Well, not something, rather, someone that has been in a thorn in my side and my wallet for too long."

"Interesting," she said, stroking her chin gently with the sharpened metal. "And why is it so urgent that this…

112

person, needs to be taken care of?"

"Well, admittedly, I had intended to ask for your assistance in ridding me of nuisances he causes me while I traveled to the Kunasai. But, in light of recent developments, I have found that my journey to the southern empire will not be warranted. So, instead of canceling the entire expedition, I saw an opportunity to use it as a cover for my problems to disappear. The only problem is the boat that was to ferry me to the coast will be leaving in the morning. Hence why I have come so desperately seeking your help in the matter."

"Hmm, what was your purpose for going to Kunasai so late in the season? Has someone decided to enter into the big boy world of trade?" she teased, but there was no true humor in her smile.

My father, who failed to see through her faux emotions, let out a chuckle and nodded, replying: "Truthfully, yes."

"Very interesting. Does this happen to do with you marrying off your daughter to that fat pig Vor'Kaige?"

My father was taken aback at her words, blurting out: "How did you know about that?"

"Oh, Rither. You do realize Cynric has his hands in the pockets of all the, for a lack of better word, unique trading within the city, right?"

At the mention of the name Cynric, my father visibly paled.

"I'll take that as a no," she said as she walked around the desk to sit upon its edge closest to my father. "In regard to your current predicament, I suppose I could lend a hand."

The color returned to my father's face, and he had moved to thank her, but Jazmin raised her un-clawed hand stopping him.

"Hold on. You might not want to thank me just yet, as it will not be cheap. Especially in order to gather enough men for whatever it is you have planned. But I must tell you, I will be informing Cynric of your recent introduction to our world. So, I would expect that a meeting with him will soon be happening. And let me warn you, Cynric is not someone who handles contemptuous comments nearly as well as I do. Do what you will with that information, it matters not to me. I still get paid regardless." Then she stood, and circled him, dragging a clawed finger over the top of his clothing before stopping beside him. "Now, let us see what men I can round up while we discuss the finer details of our business dealing. Then we can go about taking care of..." she trailed off, looking expectantly at my father.

"Trevan," he replied bluntly.

Jazmin let a truly evil smile cross her face and said

something to my father. But, once I heard my uncle's name leave his lips, the vision became muddled as a sharp ringing overtook all of my senses and everything faded completely.

CHAPTER 12

"No!" I screamed, abruptly sitting up as my room snapped back into existence around me, the ringing in my ears intensifying for a heartbeat.

As it faded, the sudden movement jostled Fi awake, and she let out a surprised yelp. It was quickly followed by another as she was forced into a sitting position, and fell off the side of the bed, landing on her butt with a thump. As I looked down at her I winced, having forgotten she was there.

"What was that fer?" she complained, as she untangled her feet from the blanket that had covered the two of us.

"Sor -" I began to reply, but the shock of my father's intentions for my uncle hit me again, and my panic returned in full swing.

"Oh gods. Oh gods, no!" I threw the rest of the blanket off me and stood.

"What's wrong?" Fi asked, a look of confusion and concern on her face.

"Uncle Trevan." I began pacing, before breaking into hysterical muttering. "How could he do that? What is he even thinking!?"

At the mention of my uncle, Fi's face became a mirror of my own panic, and she began frantically searching the room for something, what it was I didn't know. "Master Trevan? He's coming? Oh gods, I can't let him find me again. Not after last time."

"Sending him off to Kunasai is one thing, but this…" I trailed off, remembering the woman Jazmin and the fear she'd struck in my father. "Who even were those people? That woman, Jazmin, and Lohan, they're clearly not good. The way she intimidated him… I mean, yeah, I was always assumed father was somehow involved in the illegal side of Amaford, but hiring those… those thugs, that's beyond what I thought that monster was capable." I continued, failing to hear or see Fi's terror as I continued trying to make sense of my father's actions in the vision.

"Wait…" Fi said, stopping her search and turning to observe my hysterics. "Monster? Master Trevan?"

"And in the morning no less. All for what? To keep him from protecting me from that disgusting pig?" I ranted, my panic giving way to the roiling rage I felt for my father.

"Protect ya? Who's protectin' ya? And what pig?" Fi echoed, before stepping in front of me and putting her hands upon my chest. "Aubviel, what is goin' on?"

I glared at her for a breath, then screamed, "My father is going to have Trevan killed! All so he doesn't interfere with his plans to marry me off!"

My reaction hit Fi like a slap, and she stumbled back a few steps while her mouth dropped, and her eyes widened to the point of popping out of her skull. "Wha-what?"

Stepping up to her, I placed my hands roughly on her shoulders and leveled my face with hers. "My father, at dinner informed me that I was to wed a vile man from the Southern Empire, and that he was sending my Uncle Trevan to the city of Kunasai within the Southern Empire on a business venture. But it was all bullshit. He's sending Trevan but has no intention of letting him ever arrive there. He plans to have him killed on board ship."

Fi flinched as I my fingers dug into her. Despite that, she was able to meekly reply, "He told ya this?"

"Well…" I paused, releasing her, and sat heavily upon the bed. "No. He didn't tell me exactly. But I did see and hear him meet with some unsavory people seeking their help."

At those words, Fi's expression changed to one of confusion, tilting her head slightly as she stared at me. "Weren't ya jus' sleepin'? 'Cause I never felt ya get up."

"No, and yes. I guess." I hesitated, wondering if I should even bother trying to explain it to her. "It was like a dream, but I was somewhere else. Somewhere where I could experience everything, even down to the smells of the place," I partially explained.

Her face softened and I already knew what she was going to say as her smile gave her intentions away. "Oh, Aubviel -" she began, but I cut her off.

"It wasn't a dream, Fi: I'm telling you the truth. I even saw my uncle passed out in a carriage as he left for the docks."

Undeterred by my interruption, Fi continued to smile and gently sat beside me. She spoke as she placed her hand on mine, "I'm sure they seemed real, and I know that ya believe they were. But they couldn' have been, because ya were here with me." She then placed her head on my shoulder and began speaking softly. "I've had dreams like that before, too. Dreams that felt so real, that it was like they actually happened. It wasn' 'til I opened my eyes the next mornin' that I realized it had all been within my head."

"No. No, it couldn't have been a dream. I've had dreams that felt real, but this was something completely different. It's as if I was somewhere else. I can't explain it. Not without you thinking I'm crazy." I shook my head, denying Fi's logical explanation.

"I don' think ya crazy." Her soothing tone reminded me of Engrid when she tried to comfort me as a child. "I'm sure that master Trevan bein' sent away, and ya impendin'..." she paused, before forcing the words out, "marriage, was a shock. But I think ya might jus' be confused and feelin' strong emotions from ya father's news. Because o' that, it was reflected in ya dreams is all."

"Ugh! I sat up, once again knocking the girl off me, and began my pacing anew. "I know it sounds crazy, I know there is a logical explanation, but that's not what it was. It *was* real. I know it was."

The repeated disregard for her presence must have been enough to spark ire because what she said next was laden with attitude. "Even if it were real, what could ya do about it? It's not like ya can just run off and stop the whole thing."

"Wait," I said, stopping her. "That's exactly what I should do."

"What? No, that's not what I mea -"

"I could go down to the docks, sneak onto the boat, and warn Uncle Trevan," I said, speaking my thoughts aloud,, as I stripped off my nightwear and rushed to my armoire. "Yes, that'll work. I just need to get out of the house before father returns, run down to the docks and warn him before they set off."

The spark of hope ignited something within me, and I hurried to grab the outfit I normally wore for training with my uncle - a pair of tight-fitting trousers, a plain cotton shirt and my worn leather boots. I was already pulling the shirt over my head when Fi finally spoke again:

"Aubviel, are ya mad?"

"Despite what you might think, no, I'm not," I replied as my head poked through the top and I threaded my arms into the garment.

"Really?" Her haughty tone caught my attention.

Turning towards her, I noticed that she stood with her eyebrows raised and her mouth pursed to one side, staring at me with obvious skepticism. If I was being honest with myself at that moment, it made her appear cute. Because of this, I let out a sigh and approached, taking her hands in mine while looking deep into her eyes.

"Look, I don't have much time. But you must believe me that this is real." Searching her eyes for any sign of that she might relent her opposition. Finding none, I continued, hoping that I could get through to the girl. "Even if what I experienced was a dream. I won't be able to live with myself if it turned out to be real. Uncle Trevan is the only real family I have left. I can't sit back and do nothing if his life really is in danger. Can you at least try to understand that?" I finished, placing a hand on her cheek and caressing it gently.

My touch caused Fi's determination to falter, and she let out a huff. "I can't. As I have no family anymore. Here is the closest thing ta family I've had in a long time. Yaself included in that. I-I just…" she trailed off as tears collected in the corner of her eyes. "I just don' want anythin' ta happen ta ya."

"Nothing will happen. I promise. I just need to make sure my uncle is safe. That's all."

"And if ya were wrong, and it was jus' a dream after all?"

"Then I'll turn right around and come home. Honestly, I hope that's the case. But I can't risk it."

As we stood there, I couldn't help the small part of me that wanted to just pull her into my arms and return to bed. But I knew I couldn't. I knew that I wasn't crazy, and that my uncle was actually in trouble. That my father was evil and she'd yet to truly experience it since she came here. That he would go to any length to achieve his obsession with money and the sadistic power that came with it. Even if it meant killing off his only brother.

After a time, Fi's gaze dropped, and I knew I had won the moment. I pulled her against me and whispered, "Thank you" into her ear. I continued to hug her tightly for a long moment, before letting her go and holding her at arm's length.

"Truly, Fi. Thank you. I know you don't truly understand. But I promise I'll be back soon."

"Ya better. Or I won' forgive ya, ya know."

I let out a gentle smile, "I know. But you can tell me how dumb I am after I get back." Then I looked around the room, before facing her again. "I really need to go though. I need to leave before my father returns."

"I know…" she said, looking down again, her worry all but radiating off her. "Go then. Before I try and stop ya again."

Lifting her head, I pressed my lips to hers. She hesitated at first but quickly returned my kiss with fervor. I felt a warmth rise inside me, and I had to break away from her or risk getting lost in my desire. As I did, she looked at me longingly and I gave her a grin. "You can have me all to yourself when I get back."

"I'll hold ya ta that," she teased. Then as if remembering why I was leaving, her attitude reverted back to that of worry.

My heart ached at seeing her that way, but I knew I was just wasting time. So, with another quick kiss, I turned and made my way to the door. When I did, a moment of dread washed through me, as I remembered there was supposed to be a servant posted outside my room. But, as I cracked the door open, I was relieved to see that no one was present.

Creaking the door open further, I looked back at Fi and smiled.

"Be careful," she whispered.

"I will," I replied, shutting the door quietly behind me.

CHAPTER 13

I left my room, heading for the servant's area as I knew most of the staff would be asleep by that point. That, and if my father did happen to come home, he'd never enter through that section of the house without a purpose. His ego and pride would never allow such an indignity as being found within the helps' domain of the house. In fact, the only times he'd ever stepped foot into their area were when I had been hiding from him. Even then, it was always a last resort, as he would more often send one of the servants, or my uncle, to get me. But, if he had to come find me within their quarters, it meant I was in a world of trouble.

So, I knew it would be my best shot at getting out of the house without being seen. And for the most part I was correct, since I only had to pause once in my journey when two women in the kitchen were chatting over washing the staff's dishes.

It always surprised me how late they ate, but I also knew that my father was very adamant that they did not do so before him. So, it normally resulted in the staff having pre-made dishes, or late dinners on the occasions where they could dine together. So, as I stopped, waiting for an opportune time to continue, I couldn't help but overhear their conversation.

"… that such a beautiful girl should be shipped off to marry that vile man," one of them said.

"Gods be with the girl! She's had a hard life. Growin' without her mother and fathered by such a violent man. Only to be thrust into a marriage to a man none the less!" the other added.

"A shame. She deserves better than that."

"Aye."

"That reminds me, did you hear? Master Trevan is being sent to the southern Empire?" the first spoke again.

"What!"

"Yup, ships off in the mornin,' so he won't even be able to protest the wedding in Aubviel's interest. Gods, that man is a saint. It's too bad he's a poof. A man like that would make the perfect husband."

I heard the second woman gasp, and then was followed by, "Vivian!" which sent the aforementioned woman into a fit of giggles. It was soon echoed by the first, and I knew it was my time to move.

After that, it wasn't much farther to go before I came to the servants' entrance. From there it would lead me to the small stable that housed the few horses we owned, along with a carriage that would most likely be missing, as it was my father's preferred way to travel throughout the city if his destination was beyond comfortable walking distance. If he had infact taken the carriage, it would mean there would be one of our three horses still available, as the carriage took two of them to pull it. In truth, I felt bad for the animals, since they were not used often, and not without the carriage. The horses, as with most of the things my father insisted on having, had more to do with the appearance of wealth than they did with practicality, though, that did not stop me from learning how to ride. This was in no small part to Dannin, who had taken it upon himself to teach me.

He'd once explained that he had experience with horses before coming into our service and offered to teach me how to ride and care for the animals. Because of this, he ended up being the de facto stable master on top of his household duties. But he seemed to genuinely enjoy the work, as I had never heard him complain about the added responsibilities. I just hoped the man wouldn't be waiting for my father to return.

It wasn't that I didn't trust Dannin to keep my escape secret. In fact, he was one of the three servants I genuinely cared for beyond their employment to my father. Dannin and Engrid had been constant presences throughout my life, and I loved them as I would close relatives. Mainly, this was because they had raised me with a more paternal affection than my father's censorious domination ever had. But that didn't mean I wished to explain myself to the man.

The gods must not have been looking out for me because as I opened the door leading outside, I noticed a soft glow from the small window at the stable's side door, which meant someone was within. So, I slowed my approach further, and began creeping along the pathway towards the wooden building. The stable building consisted mainly of wood, and even though it was well constructed, I could still make out light coming from the small cracks in its exterior. Other than the door ahead, there were two large sliding doors at the front, which was proceeded by a gravel path leading to the main street. They were currently out of my view, but I had no doubt they'd been opened recently as Dannin would leave them open during the summer months to keep some semblance of airflow within the cramped area. Beyond that, the exterior had a handful of shuttered windows, and a side door, which I was walking towards.

I couldn't make out much through the small window. The light from within, paired with the darkness of the night made it too difficult to make out any details within. Not that I truly needed any help with the layout, as it too had a similarly simple design. But, despite its bare design it did have enough room to house the carriage, where it could be maintained and stored when not in use.

The carriage was exactly what I was looking for as I quietly neared the building. It wasn't until I was a few feet away from the small window that I was able to recognize anything specific inside. So, I readied myself to carefully peer inside when I felt a hand wrap around my waist and quickly yank me away. A scream was already building in my throat when a second hand covered my mouth. At this point panic began to set in and I fought against my abductor. It wasn't until they had pulled me away from the window's line of sight that I felt someone's mouth all but touch my ear and a familiar voice whisper.

"I don't know why you're here. But your father and a very dangerous woman are inside the stables." Dannin's breathy, barely audible voice reached my ear.

The panicked thought of being assaulted ceased, and I relaxed in Dannin's strong grip. Once I'd calmed enough, he released me, and I whirled on him. I had full intentions of

131

smacking the bigger man, but as I faced him, he lifted a finger to his lips for silence. He then emphasized his meaning by pointing towards the stables and his words sank in.

My eyes went wide as realization struck me. The dangerous woman Dannin was referring to could only be one person, Jazmin. Then, I couldn't help but wonder why my father would ever bring that woman to our home. Dannin must have mistaken my recognition for genuine surprise because all he did in response was crook a finger at me, indicating I should follow him. Not knowing what else I should do, I nodded and followed behind him as he silently made his way behind the stable to an open window.

Once there, he stopped, and indicated I should do the same. Then he held a cupped hand behind his ear, and I nodded once again. As I did, I knew instantly as to why he'd made the motion.

"While I appreciate your last-minute accommodations. I don't see why you felt it necessary to join me on the return trip to my home." My father's barely contained irritation echoed out of the window.

I could hear the scuffling of my father's boots on the dirt ground, as nothing but silence followed his statement. It wasn't until he stopped moving did someone answer. The cold female voice that answered sent ice through my veins and I latched onto Dannin's arm to prevent myself from fleeing.

"As lovely as your company has been, Rither." Jazmin, whose voice that had been forever burned into my memory, spoke. "Your comfort isn't my concern."

"I ..." My father started, his voice rising, but stopped just as he'd spoken. There was a pause, then with a more collected tone he began again. "I just worry about your presence being noticed by those surrounding families."

There was a scoff from Jazmin, then she answered: "Please, half of the district has their businesses tied up with Cynric. No one would risk their..." she trailed off, and a rapid series of metallic clacking rang through the building as she continued, "standing with him, by raising any fuss at my presence."

I thought I heard my father gulp, but I couldn't be sure if I'd heard correctly. Then, after another pause in the conversation my father probed, his tone tentative: "So, why did you accompany me?"

"Well..." her voice became more muffled as she moved away from the window. I then heard the horses begin to shift within their stalls, and the dull thuds as they pawed the ground, before I heard Jazmin speak again. "Since I've yet to receive payment for our dealings, I'm going to need some sort of collateral from you. And, what better than your horse? I'm not about to walk all the way back tonight."

"Do you not trust my word as a tradesman?"

This brought a burst of laughter from the woman, but it was anything but mirthful. "I trust no man. But I have no doubt you'll pay what is due. Even if you didn't, Cynric has ways to get what is owed him."

"Then …" My father started but was cut off.

"It's simply a show of faith in our ability to deliver. You have nothing to worry about, since the horse will be returned to you once we have received your first payment. If not - well, I'll be returning it personally." Her threat was evident even though I barely made out her words over the noise of the nervous horse's movements.

"Right, I understand," my father replied, his tone just as nervous as the horses pacing within their stalls. "Uh. Let me fetch Dannin, and I'll have him prepare one of the horses for you."

Dannin, who'd I'd been pressed up against while listening, stiffened, and turned to head back the way we'd come. As he did, I put a hand on his arm to stop him. But he just shook his head and leaned in closer. "I told your father I'd be back to bed the horses. It's been too long. I need to return."

I strengthened my grip on him for a moment, not wanting him to put himself in further danger by spending any more time around that woman than he had to. But the pleading look in his eyes spoke louder than any words. So, with much trepidation, I released his arm after giving it a quick squeeze.

As Dannin turned and left, I heard Jazmin reply to my father's offer, "No need. I'm well versed in tacking a horse. Unlike the folk we do business with, I prefer to manage things myself." And despite the seriousness of the situation, I let a smile slip onto my face as I watched Dannin head back towards the door I had almost foolishly entered.

While I watched him go, I couldn't help but feel immense gratitude towards the man. For if it had not been for Dannin, I'd have walked blindly into a situation far worse than I could have imagined, because, as far as my father was concerned, I was dutifully sleeping within my room, stewing in the fate he'd forced on me. So, if I had waltzed in, looking the part of a runaway, I had no doubt that it would have ended in a serious beating from him. That thought stirred the rage buried within me, and in that moment, I apologized to Dannin for what I was about to do, because it was by far, one of the dumbest decisions I'd ever made in my life.

CHAPTER 14

"Dannin, it's about damn time you got back," is what I heard my father say before I whipped open the stable door, slamming it against the exterior of the building. The noise made everyone stop and look towards the now open door.

My father's face was riddled with confusion at the sudden interruption, where Jazmin showed almost complete indifference besides a slight smirk as she ran a hand down one of our horse's muzzle, calming it. Meanwhile, utter terror blanched Dannin's face as his eyes met mine. This normally would have broken my rage-fueled actions, but enough was enough. It was high time someone stood up to the monster that was my father. And who better than me, the daughter he'd so casually abused and controlled her entire life? The daughter who had just wanted to happily love those around her and was punished for something that was completely out of her control. The daughter he was planning to marry off to a vile man just so he could have more meaningless power within a twisted society. So, on the eve of my beloved uncle's planned murder, I was ready to take control of the life that had been held out of my reach.

"How dare you!" I screamed, taking a step forward into the stables.

Recognition flitted across my father's face, and then turned to a rage matching my own. "Aubviel! What in the hells do you think you're doing? Get back inside where you belong."

Jazmin turned her attention towards me and took a casual stance as I felt more than saw her eyes assessing me from across the room. Dannin all but stumbled forward, trying to step between my father and me, his hands raised towards him. "Sir, I don't know why Miss Aubviel is here. But I'll make sure she gets back to her room."

My father ignored his protest by stepping forward and moving him aside with one arm, "No, I'll deal with this ungrateful little bitch myself."

Dannin dutifully stood aside, as my father approached me, and I saw a mix of emotions cross the his face as he was conflicted about what to do. Meanwhile Jazmin's smirk twisted into a scowl at my father's words, and I saw her hand tighten on the reins she'd procured while tacking up the animal.

"Tell me, Aubviel, what is it I dare do? Hmm?" My father seethed, as he slowly march towards me continued.

"You know exactly what I'm talking about."

"Ha!" he barked out. "There are many things you could be referring to. But please, enlighten me on what atrocity I've committed that brings you from the comforts of our home."

"Oh, don't you even fucking think about trying to act like you're the victim here. You sick son of a bitch!"

This caused my father to momentarily stop, and he started quivering as his face turned a bright red. "What did you just say to me?"

"You heard me." I stood my ground, even though my conditioned response was to cower away from him.

"Who the hells do you think you are, little girl?" His voice was more of a growl.

"The one person to stand up for those lives you plan on ruining."

"As if you have a choice! I am your father. You owe me your gods damn life, and it's time for me to capitalize on it by marrying you off."

"Fuck you!" I spat, my body likewise quivering in

unadulterated rage. "And what of Trevan? Huh? What about his life? Is it really worth the coin you're paying that woman to end it?"

Behind my father, I saw Dannin's eyes go wide, as he stood, frozen in shock and fear. Meanwhile, Jazmin had released the horse's reins and came to stand in the middle of the stables, watching with increased interest as she crossed her arms and smiled.

"How could you have possibly known about that?" he asked, turning towards Dannin with violence in his eyes. "Did you tell her?"

"Leave him alone. He didn't need to tell me anything about the pathetic sack of shit you are!" I spat in Dannin's defense.

"Insult me one more time, and you'll regret the moment you opened your eyes," my father replied.

"Oh, like that is supposed to scare me. Have you forgotten? You've been beating me since I was a child. Well, I'm here now to say it's time that ends." I stood taller, my eyes narrowing as I projected my hatred out towards him.

"Apparently not enough," he said, as he lunged the last few feet between us, his fist clenched and pulled back for a punch.

I'm not sure what exactly triggered my next actions, but my body began moving on its own as I ducked into a crouch and extended my arms out wide. At the same time, I pivoted my body, spinning just enough that my father's momentum sent him off balance and he stumbled past me. Following through with the movement, I came back up in a ready stance, and waited as my father whipped himself around to face me once again. He breathed heavily through his nose, as his eyes began to redden and bulge, resembling a wild boar more than a man. Then, like the animal he resembled, he let out a frustrated grunt and charged at me.

The reckless display was almost pitiful, and I felt a smile cross my face as I easily spun out of the way, clenching my fist into a ball and striking him in the back of the head as I completed my rotation. The blow caused him to stumble face first into the ground and there was audible "oof" as he skidded to a stop on his stomach. It was then I began to realize what was happening to me, and why I was able to so deftly defend against the beast before me. It was fear. The fear I had for my father was being drowned out by the utter disdain I held for the man. That, and the physical training my uncle had instilled in me through our sparring was coming to fruition as my body fell into the familiarity of the fray. It was if I didn't even need to think about what to do, my body knew how and when to react on its own. That training was what made countering my father's feeble and clumsy attacks so easy. So, I stood, watching while it took a moment longer than it should have for my father to right himself, and I let my grin of satisfaction spread further as I noticed his chest heaving from his effort.

Pushing his out of shape body up, a body that had not been used for any sort of physical activity in countless years, my father looked at Dannin and snarled: "Are you just going to stand there? Or has fucking my brother all these years made you forget who employs you?"

Dannin, who was still too taken aback by the sudden flurry of the situation, stared mindlessly between my father and me in indecision. As he struggled to process what to do, I took the liberty to answer in his stead: "You insult Uncle Trevan, like he's something lesser than you because of his attraction to men. But who truly is the lesser man between you two? The man that fights and cares for his loved ones? Or the man who's gotten too fat from a life of smoke and mirrors that he cannot even stand to fight his own daughter alone?"

"You little bitch. You grow some semblance of a spine, and think that is going to change your fate? I will get my way. Trevan will be dead, and you'll be shipped off to Vor'Kaige to do as he pleases. I don't care if I must send you to him in a heap, it'll just make it that much easier for him to fuck you into submission." His threatening words were nothing more than empty syllables to me as I watched him struggle to control his breathing. I knew he was spouting off insults as a last-ditch effort to shake my confidence, but he was sorely mistaken as I saw the demon I had feared all my life for what it truly was: a pathetic man who'd gripped so tightly to power through violence and terror that he'd snapped the control he possessed in his struggle to keep it.

I just smiled back at the wretched man and relaxed my posture as I knew I'd finally won. "I don't think so, father. You've lost all power over me, and I'll never allow you to take that control back."

"I'll fucking kill you," he said in a quiet snarl. But as he did so, his eyes went wide as a clawed hand reached around from behind and placed bladed fingers forcefully upon his neck. The pressure from the blades that were pressing into my father's skin and caused rivulets of blood to run down his neck. The threat of actual pain caused him to straighten, and his body went rigid.

"Ah, ah, ah. I don't think so Rither." Jazmin said coolly behind my father.

"What... What are you doing?" Shock etched on his face at the unexpected development.

"Do you want my professional or personal answer?"

"I don't understand. I thought we had a deal. Why

are you attacking me?"

"Well. What I'll be telling Cynric is that I was simply protecting a potential long-term asset. But, in truth, I'm just doing the world a favor by taming a rabid animal that needs to be caged," she replied.

"How… how dare you! We made a fucking deal!" my father managed to croak out through her grip.

"For which I have yet to provide any sort of service. Plus, have I seen any sort of payment? No, no I haven't."

"Cynric will hear of this! I will make sure he knows what type of dealings you do under his name," he threatened.

"And that, my dear Rither, was exactly the wrong thing to say," she said, ripping her clawed hand viciously across his neck, cutting my father's throat open in a spray of blood. "Because he'll never even know you existed."

My father let out a gurgling choke as he grasped at his throat in a frantic attempt to staunch the bleeding. But the wounds were too deep and he stumbled forward as his heart continued to pump blood through his severed neck. The violence, paired with the metallic scent of blood filling the air, sent the horses into a panic. They began to buck against their stalls and whined loudly as my father dropped on the ground, blood foaming from the wound as his lungs filled with the liquid he was so desperate to stop. After a moment, he lay motionless, his hands still around his neck as the steady flow of blood began pooling in front of his body.

I, along with Dannin, stared mutely at the still warm body of the man that had been nothing but a constant source of fear and pain in our lives. But, even as I stared at the sight of my father dead before me, I was unable to drum up any one specific emotion. On one hand I was thankful and relieved that his tyranny had ended. But I was also afraid of why Jazmin had killed him so sudden, so ruthlessly. All I could think to do was raise my eyes to the woman who'd just saved and possibly damned me to a life within the city's dungeons.

The intention of my stare must have been obvious as Jazmin shrugged. "A man like your father is bound to cause endless problems, and trample over any who might get in his way. That, dear child, is not a person you want to be in business with. Plus, had I known the true intentions of your proposed marriage, I would have turned him away immediately, fuck the potential financial gain. Slavery is one thing, but even my blurred lines can be crossed on occasion. Plus, after your display, I realized I liked your spunk. Couldn't see that be wasted so carelessly." Then, with clearly practiced ease, clapped her hands, despite the danger her claws posed. "Right. Dannin, would you be a dear and help me ready the carriage once more?"

Dannin, slowly turned to gape at the woman, then back down to my father's body.

"Oh, don't worry about him. Once we have retrieved Trevan from the port, I will have my men follow us back and take care of the mess."

Her nonchalant attitude was unsettling to say the least. But Dannin slowly moved from the spot he was rooted to and began the task of readying the horses.

After Jazmin spoke, I scrunched my eyes in confusion, saying: "Retrieve Trevan? Are you not going to kill him?"

"Why would I?" Jazmin replied, as she removed her bladed glove, and began trying to soothe the horses once again.

"But…" I trailed off.

"The person I had made that deal with is no longer breathing. There's no reason to put forth effort into something I'll not be paid for. It's not like I care whether Trevan lives or dies, but now that there's no coin involved, there's no reason to proceed as was intended." Then she turned her head towards me and raised an eyebrow. "That is, unless you still want your uncle to die?"

"No, of course I don't! I… I just didn't expect any

of this." I said, motioning to my father's body.

"And what did you expect to happen?" she stopped, turning to face me completely.

"I... I don't know."

"Well. What's done is done. Now, are you going to just stand there like a fish out of water, or are you going to help me go retrieve your uncle?"

CHAPTER 15

I was surprised at how easy it was to ignore the fact that my father had just been killed in front of me as Dannin, Jazmin and I readied the horses for the carriage. Dannin at least seemed to be relieved at being given something to do, and I still hadn't wrapped my head around the newfound freedom I'd gained from Jazmin's actions.

So, I couldn't help but stare at her as we sat inside the carriage, silently bouncing along while traversing the desolate streets. As I did, I couldn't even begin to understand why she'd done what she had. Not that I was upset that my father was dead: he deserved a fate far worse than the one dealt by her hand. But it seemed so out of character for someone so involved in the underbelly of Amaford society. Sure, she'd said that she could justify her actions to her boss by protecting future assets, whatever that was supposed to mean, but wouldn't she have gained more by letting my father live? I couldn't for the life of me begin to know what went

149

through that woman's head.

While I was not hiding my stare, when Jazmin spoke without taking her eyes off the passing houses, it took me by surprise.

"It's not as easy as you might think." Her voice was calm and relaxed, though not in the menacing way it had been earlier.

"What? Killing people?" My bluntness surprising me, as I clapped my hands over my mouth, then just as quickly removed them to apologize. "I'm sorry, that was inappropriate."

Jazmin let out a soft chuckle, and it was the first time I believed it to be genuine. "No, that part is quite easy, actually. It's hard to feel remorse for people like your father. Gods know that I deal with plenty like him, and worse." She paused for a moment and turned her head to meet my eyes. "It's not easy being a woman and maintaining the level of fear and respect I have gained within this city."

"You seem to being doing just fine to me."

She rolled her eyes and smiled, "It's been an extraordinarily long road to get to where I am now. I've been wearing this mask for so long that I often forget the person I lost within me."

150

"What do you mean?" My curiosity perked up, and I unintentionally began scooting myself closer to the woman.

"I haven't always been, this…" she paused to wave a hand at herself, "cold."

I didn't say anything, just sat and listened as she seemed to contemplate her next words, almost as if she was struggling with them. I couldn't help but wonder if it had something to do with the mask she had referred to.

Then she sighed, looking back out of the window. "I was like you once. Though our situations couldn't be any farther from each other. When I was young, I had no one. No family, friends, anyone. I got through the days by stealing and selling my body to men, at an age much younger than yourself. I know the abuse a man can inflict on a child when they believe they have absolute power over you." She went quiet, her distant expression making it clear she was not seeing our current surroundings. "I fought. And took the abuse because I didn't know any better. Eventually, I just accepted the life the gods had given me. It made me cold, angry, and yes, heartless towards others. That's why this lifestyle appears so easy for me. But, it wasn't until the day Cynric caught one of his men beating me within an inch of my life for allegedly stealing coins from him after he'd paid for my services, that things began to change. He decided then to take me under his wing and showed me a life of kindness

I didn't think existed."

I was digesting what Jazmin was saying, trying to put myself in her shoes, but couldn't begin to understand the pain she endured, then asked softly: "What happened?"

"To the man?" she turned back to me, a slight smile on her face. "I killed him."

My eyes went wide, and she laughed. "It wasn't until years later, mind you. Cynric had the man's legs broken and tossed from the organization. It wasn't until after I'd grown and gone through years of learning the basics: reading, writing, combat training, and the like, that I found him one day in South Bridge District. That's when I buried a knife into his gut and left him to bleed out like the pig he was."

"Oh." My face scrunched in confusion. "You said that it isn't easy. But even through the trials of your younger years, you speak so casually of killing."

She shrugged, "I suppose it does seem simple to an outsider. But the truth is. The little girl who was denied a life of love and affection is still in here somewhere, and every now and then…" a pained look crossed her face as she paused.

"Still yearns for the love you were denied," I whispered.

Jazmin nodded numbly, and I tentatively placed a hand on her leg. "Is that why... why you killed my father?"

She looked down at my hand, and in a moment of panic I almost pulled it away. But I managed to fight through my fear, and after a moment Jazmin placed a hand upon mine. "I suppose so."

We sat there in silence for a long while before she looked up into my eyes. "The truth is, I saw the look in your eyes back in the stables. I saw the look of hatred and violence in you. You would have killed him given the opportunity, wouldn't you?"

I thought for a moment, then nodded slightly.

"I thought so." Then she squeezed my hand slightly, "That's why I stepped in."

"What? I don't understand."

"I was saving you from having to do it yourself. I know what that can do to a person, and a girl should never have to deal with something like that by herself. It's a lot to put on the shoulders of a child. Even one of your age."

"I think I understand," I said, taking both her hands in mine and pulled them between us while looking her straight in the eyes. As I did, I saw the surprised look in her face as I spoke again. "But like you had to do for yourself. I would do anything to keep those I care about safe, and they would do the same for me. I appreciate what you did for me back there, I do. But I would have found a way to get through it. At least now, I know my uncle is safe, and that is what is most important to me."

Jazmin's surprise faded, and it transitioned into a genuine smile, "I can understand that. That is how I feel about Cynric."

"He's that important to you?"

"Of course. He's like a father to me. I'm guessing your uncle is something similar?"

"Yes. He's the complete opposite of my father in every way."

"Well, I'm sorry then."

"For what?" I asked.

"For putting his life in danger. It was me and my men who were going to take his life. Or have you forgotten that in our chat?" she said, a mischievous smile replacing her previous one.

"Oh, I haven't forgotten. You still scare the ever-living crap out of me." I grinned back.

"Good, can't let my reputation slip, you know," she

said, before removing her hands from mine, and she looked at me with intrigue. "Speaking of your uncle - back at the stables, you claimed to have known about your father and I's plan to have him killed. How is that?"

For a moment, I debated on telling Jazmin the truth. But I decided it might be best to play it off as a fanciful coincidence, as that's how it would appear to others based on Fi's reactions. "To be honest, it was a bit of a stretch, and embarrassingly enough, a gross overreaction to a dream I had earlier. I dreamed of my father sending out an order to have Trevan killed. That, paired with his supposed departure tomorrow, and my father announcing my marriage, my emotions were running a bit high. So, I couldn't stand idly by and risk the chance that my father had actually done such a thing."

Jazmin's eyebrow rose, and I got the impression that she didn't believe me. But she didn't press further, just responded with a deadpan "Emotions of a young girl."

"Exactly," I smiled back at her. But any sense of her previous warmth was gone as she glanced out the window.

"We'll be there soon. Let me lead, and don't go running off right away. My men have been ordered to handle any interlopers harshly."

My smile faded as the mask she'd mentioned settled

back onto her features, and it broke my heart at seeing the change. So, I placed a hand on her leg and squeezed, "Jazmin. I can't thank you enough for what you've done for me and my uncle. Truly."

Other than a slight twitch on the side of her mouth, she gave no indication of having any emotional response to my gratitude. "There's nothing to thank me for. I simply found you and your uncle to be the more potentially profitable choice."

"Still…" I added, smiling softly as I saw her eyes dart towards me for a second before the carriage came to a complete stop.

"We're here. Stay close and be quiet. I'll handle my men," she said, before proceeding to exit

I wiped the smile from my face, lowered my head, and quietly did what I was told by following behind her. Even if all I wanted to do was sprint towards the docks and wrap my uncle in the biggest hug possible.

EPILOGUE

The candlelight flickered off the weathered wood of the cabin, as I sat upon a cushioned chair in front of a simple writing desk. Both the desk and chair had been bolted to the floor to prevent them from sliding or launching themselves across the room during particularly rough storms. Though, I had yet to experience anything worse than a light rainstorm as we'd set sail upon the South Sea, two days prior.

The cool salt-tinged air that drifted in through the cabin's window sent a shiver down my back as it brushed against my exposed skin, and I debated closing it. But hearing Fi's heavy breathing from the bed behind me, I didn't want to risk waking her in the process. So, I ignored the slight discomfort and shifted on the chair, focusing upon the blank parchment before me. Then I opened the small case mounted upon the desk, pulling out a small bottle of black ink and a basic quill. After placing the bottle within a grooved section of the desk that was meant for that very purpose, I dipped in the quill and began writing my letter.

Dear Sephyrl,

I feel as if I must apologize to you for not being able to say goodbye. These past couple of weeks have been quite busy and chaotic. Especially as Uncle Trevan and I have been scrambling to secure what little was left of my father's legacy after his death.

Sephryl had been told the truth of what had happened to my father. The arranged marriage, plotting my uncle's murder, his death, and all that came with it, only a handful days after it had happened. But that wasn't until it had been officially noted that my father's body had been found stripped and beaten within the South Bridge District, a few days after the events in the stable. Trevan and I had of course known that this was going to be the case, as Jazmin had explained what would transpire after we had retrieved him from the port that night. That was only after we had managed to sober him up enough to explain what my father had planned for him - that and the events that lead up to his rescue. So, it was no surprise to us when the city guard arrived at our door one morning after we had reported him missing, to inform us of his untimely demise. I was just thankful that Uncle Trevan had been the one to receive the news, because I knew I could not have portrayed any amount of feigned sadness for the death of my father as I honestly believed he deserved worse than the death he'd been given.

But the experience was an eye-opening one, as I became exposed to the world both my late father and uncle have been experiencing through their livelihood. I have learned quite a lot, and realized I knew more about the business of trading than I ever imagined I did.

Still, nothing could prepare me for the struggle we faced as we found that many of my father's contacts were unwilling to continue doing any business with my uncle. Which I think may be due to my uncle's love of seducing their sons and servants. But even these days Uncle Trevan has seemed to quell his previous flippancies, preferring the company of Dannin over the impulsive desires he often experienced while drinking. Even that has seemed to calm after my father's passing, as the stresses he caused us has all but dissipated within the household. It's almost as if a breath of fresh air has swept over the occupants of our home. There's an aura of peace that surrounds the residence, one that hasn't been seen since my mother's passing. I see it in the staff as well, mainly because they smile more than I've ever seen before.

That line made me pause, as I thought about Dannin, Engrid and of course Fi, who was sleeping not-so-soundlessly behind me. I thought of how shaken Dannin had been the night of my father's end, and how much it had impacted him the days following. He'd been quiet, quieter than usual, and I rarely saw him leave my uncle's quarters. Whether that was because he was taking solace in his safe return or trying to cope with his employer being brutally killed in front of him, I wasn't sure. But even as he started to emerge from my uncle's room more often, he rarely made eye-contact with me, and it seemed that he was generally avoided me if he could. It hurt, but I think seeing me brought back the memory of that night, so I understood why he was keeping his distance. I just hoped that upon my return, he would be the same old Dannin I had come to see as family once more. Engrid on the other hand, had taken the news of my father's death much better. She even seemed to have gained an extra pep in her step the weeks following. I think it was because she'd always been the one to witness first-hand the atrocities my father wrought upon me as a child. That, and I genuinely believe the only reason she stayed around for all those years was out of duty towards me. So, seeing the woman who'd been like a grandmother to me happy and spry, warmed my heart.

But, despite the changes that have come to the people of the house, we still had to find a way to continue bringing in coin. Uncle Trevan and I have stressed and argued many times over what we should do about it. That only escalated when I suggested that we renewed my father's original plan of going to Kunasai and establishing some sort of trade bargain with someone within the Empire. He was very much against the risk of it all, especially with the summer season being in full swing, making access to the city a gamble to begin with. That and any contacts my father had within the Empire would now be rendered useless with his death. But I think it is worth the risk, as my father was right, and the legitimate trade potential within the city has yet to be tapped.

It wasn't until I had contacted a woman in Amaford who holds considerable influence in the city, was I able to convince my uncle to allow me to begin preparing for the journey. Grant it, there are certain stipulations by involving the woman, as she's tasked herself with accompanying me and Fi to ensure our safety with her employer's contacts. That, and a bunch of other standard proceedings that come with every business dealing, such as an extremely detailed contract that favored her and her employer more than myself. But I believe it to be fair enough, and I'm honestly grateful for her assistance, as she is a woman of immense strength.

It was true. After I had produced the idea of traveling to the Southern Empire, in an attempt to establish some sort of lifeline back into my uncle and mine's newly acquired business, I had reached out to Jazmin. In doing so, I had found that not only was she impressively intimidating, but she was also extremely knowledgeable when it came to dealing in contracts and other minute details within the trading profession. In the end, she handled a majority of planning and had actually saved us on a number of necessary expenses for the journey. The only catch was, this meant we had to deal with some of the more unscrupulous characters of her organization. But, having her with us made the burden of her men almost unnoticeable as we were left more or less alone. Though, that didn't help me gain any sort of insight into understanding why Jazmin had insisted on coming herself. Especially when someone else could have represented her in the same manner.

Oh, I had forgotten to ask the last time I saw your brother. Has there been any word on finding Obis' apprentice? I heard about the fire in the Prominence when Trevan and I went to see him in order to transcribe our traveling papers. He'd said that Roland had gone missing after delivering something to that area around the same time the explosion happened. But I wasn't able to join Trevan when he picked the papers up, so I haven't heard if anything new had developed. I hope that by the time you receive this, something has been found out about what caused it and those involved.

I stopped writing for a moment, as I heard Fi begin to stir within the bed, and I turned to look at her while she blinked the sleep from her eyes and stared at me. "What are ya doin'?"

"I'm just writing to Sephyrl. I'm sorry if I woke you."

"It's not the writin', it's the fact ya aren't here in bed with me." She grinned mischievously.

I rolled my eyes at her. "I'm almost done. Just give me a moment longer."

Fi pouted but shifted deeper into the blankets and closed her eyes.

Turning back to the parchment, I took the quill back up and began finishing my letter.

Fi expresses her love, and dissatisfaction that you're taking my

162

attention away from her. So, I'll wrap this up. I hope that you find yourself well, and I cannot wait to hear and share stories when I get back.

Yours truly,

Aubviel

After I had finished, I set the quill down and began reading over what I had written. Satisfied, I started to fold the parchment, readying it to be placed within my bag so I could have it sent off when we hit port. But, as I was about to put it within, the tattered leather-bound journal Sephryl had given me slid out of the pack. Picking it up, I stared at its weathered bindings, and wondered when I had put it in there, as I hadn't remembered doing so. Then, just when I was about to place it back safely within my bag, I had a thought. Grabbing the letter; I unfolded it and added:

P.S.

There's a boy, almost a month back, that had been chased by the guards within the Arc District. I was wondering if you could do me the favor of finding anything out about him. I'm not exactly sure why, but I feel like the journal you gave me might be important to him.

With that, I nodded to myself and waited a moment for the ink to dry. Then I refolded the parchment and placed it in my bag. After all was set and done, I replaced my writing utensils, locking them back up so they wouldn't be jostled on ship's voyage. Once done, I arched my back, locking my fingers and stretched them above my head to ease the muscles that had begun to stiffen while I wrote.

"Ya ever comin' back to bed, or do I need to drag ya butt over 'ere?" Fi spoke up, her head peeking out from underneath the blankets.

Laughing, I rolled my eyes once more at the girl. "You know, if no one knew better, they'd think I was the one being dragged halfway across the world on your behalf."

Fi's head popped completely out of the blanket, and then she threw them aside completely, exposing the nakedness she'd hid within, her face a mockery of rage, exclaiming: "What! ya aren'? The audacity of it all! Quick, I must inform the crew that we 'ave ta turn around immediately, I can' 'ave my reputation sullied by such filth in my room."

"Oh, will you shut up! " I teased back, sliding into the bed beside her and wrapping her tightly in my arms. Then, as our bodies pressed into each other, I kissed her deeply.

After long display of shared affection, we had parted and she looked at me. There was mischief in her eyes, which seemed to be present more and more often since the beginning of our journey. "So that's what it takes ta get ya in bed. If that's the case..." she paused, then let out a loud,

"Guards!"

Thinking quickly, I kissed her again, if only to keep her quiet for the moment. Then, she burst into a fit of giggles as I began tickling her as punishment. After a moment of her begging me to stop, I lay my head back on the pillow while she flopped hers upon my chest.

"I'm glad you came," I said to her as I ran my fingers through her hair.

"Mmm. Me too," she replied, as I felt her body relax against mine, and her breathing begin to deepen.

It wasn't long before she was back asleep, and I just lay there breathing in the scent of her sweat dampened hair. As I did, I quietly reflected on what had happened to bring me to this point in my life: the people, the moments, and the hardships we'd endured throughout it all. I let a smile dominate my face as I could never have imagined in a hundred years that I'd be heading across the world with a girl I was quickly falling in love with, just to secure our livelihood in a country that was so different than my own. It was in that moment, I realized that I was finally happy – living the life I'd always read about in my fanciful books. So, as I closed my eyes, I knew that the dreams that were to come couldn't compare to the joy I was feeling at that time. All I knew was I never wanted it to end.

MORE BY THIS AUTHOR

Trials of Amaford

How Not To Be A Rogue

(A Trials of Amaford Novella, Book 1)

How Not To Be A Scribe

(A Trials of Amaford Novella, Book 2)

Charlie the Cupid

Quarter One

(Charlie the Cupid collection, Book 1)

Don't Fret! There is much more to be seen of

Amaford!

For more about me, updates on what's next for our beloved city, what I'm up to, reviews, or just to show a little love you can find me on Facebook, or My Website

zackbrooksauthor.wixsite.com/zbrooksauthor

If you enjoyed this story, please don't hesitate to leave a review.

ALSO AVAILABLE FROM GOLD DUST PUBLISHING

- The House on Dead Man's Curve
  By J. S. Roach

- Until Death: An Eric Kent Investigation – Case 1
  By Rey Nichols

- Reflections – Our charity book featuring over 40 authors contributing.

- The Purple Menace and the Tobacco Prince
  By Wade Beauchamp

- The Sword's Secret: Ancient Wonders – Book 1
  By Chris Cole

- The Vampire Crusades: The Acquisition – Book 1
  By J.S. Roach

- Mr. Tingles' Mysteries: The Curious Case of the Bodiless Head
  By Sean D. Roach

- Children of Solitude
  By Michael G. Williams

- Trial by Fire: An Eric Kent Investigation – Case 2
  By Rey Nichols

- Queer Power: Escaping the Fright
  Various Authors